Praise for Colin O'Sullivan

"A hard, poignant novel of great humanity…remarkably well written…"

—Rolling Stone (France)

"O'Sullivan's voice—unique, strong, startlingly expressive—both comes from and adds to Ireland's long and lovely literary lineage. Like many of that island's sons and daughters, O'Sullivan sends language out on a gleeful spree, exuberant, defiant, ever-ready for a party. Only a soul of stone could resist joining in."

—Niall Griffiths

"His words swagger with purpose, never meandering too long on a scene, always moving the story forward, even when it goes back in time, like a faded photograph coming into view. Lyrical to a point, one word flowing to the next, hardly stopping. I read this novel and saw a movie in my mind – that's how each page appeared to me – and that's a good thing. This story reminded me of a beautiful vase, now shattered to pieces on the floor. But with each piece picked up and glued back into place, a narrative came into being, with each piece representing a character, beautifully written with all their flaws and realism, broken by their own imperfections and weaknesses. But most of all, the dropping of the vase, once beautiful, representing by the act of a man, long gone, though his actions reverberate through the years, waiting, waiting for those sunny days in Killarney, when the sun finally gets to shine on that long buried seed, giving it the energy it needs to bloom – for good, and for evil."

—Love, Sex & Other Dirty Words

"A cathartic novel that ultimately creates positive emotions, like the blues can do. Poignant."

—Book Node

"A luminous novel that chases away the darkness…All its characters are at a crossroads and they will either meet the Devil himself or find a way towards a new life."

—Appuyez sur la touche lecture

"Carried by a genuine writing talent, *Killarney Blues* is a Noir novel full of melancholy and unfulfilled dreams with a surprising glimmer of hope at the end. Without the slightest naivety. A revelation."

—Le Soir (Belgium)

"*Killarney Blues* is a Noir novel – but not only – at the farthest reaches of love, desire and loss."

—Lettres d'Irlande et d'Ailleurs

"A novel of great finesse and humanity. Perhaps, sometimes, there is a glimmer of hope in the blues?"

—Action-suspence.com (Starred review)

"In a style that is sometimes luminous, sometimes direct, sometimes poetic, Colin O'Sullivan traces his narrative path, creates incredibly vivid and appealing characters and brings the reader, to the 12-bar beat of the blues, towards a heart-breaking denouement."

—Le blog du Polar de Velda

"This first Noir novel from Colin O'Sullivan is magnificent, very finely written, and profoundly sad. To be savoured while drinking a Guinness and listening to some old blues, by Muddy Waters or Bessie Smith. And if rain knocks on the window glass, like in Killarney, it's even better."

—RTL (Radio Télévision Luxembourg)

"Moving, tragic, masterly crafted."

—Lea Touch

"*The Dark Manual* is a mature rounded work, assured and confident, at times lyrical and beautiful but also punchy and sharp. […] engaging, inventive and thought-provoking."

—NewBooks.com

"Colin O'Sullivan is a lyrical master of the written word. There are sections of the book that are heart-breaking, in their emotional and physical sense of loss, and moments of humor, surprise, suspense, pure sudden horror, and stark naked joy."

—Marvin Minkler, Modern First Editions

Maiko Moans

COLIN O'SULLIVAN

First published in the English language in Dublin, Ireland, in 2025
by Betimes Books CLG

www.betimesbooks.com

ISBN 978-1-0686170-3-4

Maiko Moans is a work of fiction. Names, characters, places, and incidents are either the product of the author's imagination or are used fictitiously. Any resemblance to actual persons, living or dead, events, or locales is entirely coincidental.

Cover image © Keisot Lewap

Cover design by Masa Radanic

In memoriam
Bill Blizzard

"Yeah I recognize that girl
She stumbled in some time last loneliness"
The Birthday Party, "Deep in the Woods"

"When we cannot be delivered from ourselves, we delight in devouring ourselves."
Emil Cioran, *A Short History of Decay*

"And their deep cries crawled over the floors
Like an animal dragging a great trap"
Ted Hughes, "Lovesong"

This story will have a man who brandishes a knife.
Another man will brandish a sword.
The woman, she will moan, and she will try to make music.

And the house?
The house will utterly despise them all.

1

Always a rustling. Always something on the move. Through the undergrowth. Past leaves. Brushing against branches. Unsettling ferns.

Sometimes it's small, a mouse, a mole, or smaller still, a stag beetle on its warpath, armoured, ready.

Or bigger. Something bolder. A wild boar, a serow, some lost human on some lonesome trail … or larger yet, a deer, a bear!

And panting.

Forest things panting.

Out of breath maybe, or cooling hides with large gasps. Grunting or growling. Darktime howling. This is the way of the woods, day or night, and you will only recognize such when you encounter, head on – only ever truly recognize anything on such encounters, head on, no … no, much closer than that: the face to face.

Step away from the woods and notice the house nearby. A solitary, sombre house in silence. No lights. Nothing hums. People used to live there, but no one present now. Empty rooms, no one to potter around and upset the floorboards; the dust settles.

Where are its inhabitants? Its owners?

Where are the secrets kept?

Is everything buried around here?

The sounds of cicadas, sure, constant, sure, crickets too, but what else? The feeling that some wrong has been committed there in the thickets. Or perhaps that things were never quite right around here to begin with. The faint moonlight that casts faint light down upon the house now – is that to be its summation? Hazy. Waning. Unclear. Utterly unromantic, like everything that is in store.

In front of the door, a welcome mat. Rough. Flat. In English: *Welcome*. Simple as that. Makes the place seem open and inviting. But don't be fooled.

The solitary house solitary sits.
Or just … squats there, like a fat old frog on a hollow log, too ugly to love.
Unlived in.
Unloved, for sure, this house, such a long time.

But wait, folks are on the way! Coming soon. They can fill the place with noise. With music. Lilt and laughter, perhaps. Gaiety. It could do with something, this squatting frog.

A welcome mat right on the front porch, before the door, it must mean something. *Welcome*. But people just wipe their feet all over welcome mats … isn't that what they are for? Scraping dirty shoes, scraping soles, sullying. That's what people do to welcome mats. Step all over them.
This must all mean something.
Solitary house solitary.
Squatting frog.
This does not make for a promising start.
But it is all we've got.
It's where we are.

This beginning …

And they are coming. Coming!

2

They are in a beat-up old van and they are driving down a beat-up old road and the whole countryside looks a little beat up to the three of them.

They look exhausted, heat-beaten too. It's humid, like the devil's own saucepan has spilled its spiteful contents and its steam has enveloped the day.

The summer sun, the sticky stifle, it's not letting up any time soon. Sweat pours. Every pore. Temperatures soar.

Stifle is another new word Maiko has added to her collection.

Letting up is a newish phrase, too.

She learns. She acquires – she'll moan at the others if they don't explain things to her, and she'll moan if they do, too.

She can't win.

No one in this game does.

Her long toes on the dashboard – Jason has commented on them, on their length, she'd never even noticed. She thought all toes were like that until she compared them to his. And though his feet are longer, wide and mannish, her toes are way way longer, almost simian – his are just plain stubby.

And his running joke: *it's because you're Japanese*, as if that accounted for everything; her difference to the two males, culturally … gender … do these things matter still? Apparently so.

She's playing with her split ends now, wondering if she should cut the whole thing off. Her mess-mass of hair. Just chop violently, chop it all off.

Jason says it would be a shame, such beautiful black locks, black as horror nights – Jason is good with compliments; he's got some good smiles in his arsenal too, when he needs them – even though handsome men like him have no real recourse.

Pete says: *yeah, shave it all off. Go bald. Like Sinead in her heyday.*

Heyday.

Hay day.

They had to explain the difference to her.

Homophones.

And they had to explain that Sinead was an Irish rock singer who was bald but extremely pretty, back in the 1990s. Big doleful, soulful eyes, long lashes (even better when teary wet), smooth, small, pallid, delicate mouth … until it opened, and then unleashed! They're older, her bandmates, and they have to explain (mansplain, rocksplain) things to her often, as if she's a little dim, it's demoralising. But she knows that it's because she's Japanese, and that it's because it's all so alien to them, even though they're on *her* land and have been for some time, the cheek of them, the cheek! She thinks they're both full of shit and they both despise and are jealous of the fact that she is younger. So much younger. Tighter skin. Whiter teeth. They're as full of contradictions as anyone else, as full of … maybe that could be the new band name (they quibble about this, they quibble often). *The Contradictions.* Ladies and gentlemen will you please welcome to the stage, The Contradictions. So many arguments. No, not *quibbles* at all actually: *fights, fights,* actual *fights.* They haven't thought of a new one yet, for their new enterprise, a band name. *Band* suggests togetherness, suggests solidarity. They give off different vibes. Their trembling lives. Different vibes altogether. Actual fights!

Their names are Maiko, Jason, Pete.

The band name will have to wait. Inspiration. It will come. All good things. Or maybe it won't come (all bad things) and the search will be enough.

Maiko thinks she'll moan either way, whether things work out or whether they absolutely don't. There is never any winner. She'll have to snap out of thinking like that. Of winners and losers. Snap. Like a twig in the woods. Like it's that easy.

They've got this psychedelic rock music playing loud as they travel. *Kosmische* they called it. She knew that this was not an English word. What language then? German, she assumed.

Jason drives.

Can is the name of the band – some trippy 70s stuff, and they told her that the lead singer was Japanese. As if she was somehow to relate to this piece of information. Some cosmic connection. *Krautrock* – could you even say that these days? It sounded wrong, Jason said, but he also said that he wasn't afraid of being cancelled.

The music isn't bad, though she is hardly listening now, just hoping to get to the house as soon as possible, and shower all the grime off herself.

Grime. Another term. They told her it was *dirt* as well as a sort of *UK urban rap style.*

She's quite sick of both of them. Jason. Pete. Rocksplaining, mansplaining. But she's in a band with them. Stuck in the middle with them.

And if she didn't enjoy fucking Jason so much, she'd probably have found some other way to pass her time.

But here they are.

Road.

Unwashed.

Heat-beaten.

Maiko moans frequently about cleanliness. She won't let him near her pussy if she thinks she's smelling bad, or if he's smelling bad, but especially her, her own, the shame. Standards and all that. He doesn't give a shit, but she does. She can't go near his crotch if he's been out in the sun all day. He needs a shower. They all do. Grime. Get it off. And Grimes is this musician who was once, dating Elon Musk on and off – did he shuttle her off to space in some machine of his … she is trying to amuse herself but she is really too tired for jokes. And she doesn't want to think about Elon Musk anyway because she knows that the guy has stacks of money, which she doesn't want to think about. The having it. No, rather the *not having it*. Maiko could moan about that. How having money would be the answer to a lot of her problems, and how she could rent proper studios and proper gear – Pete says that word a lot: *proper* – but she's too damn tired and she's too damn dirty.

Filth.

Scummy.

Scum.

Are her moans moans of pleasure, or are they of despair?

How near at times, how close (makes you pull out your own hair).

Can Maiko tell what's what?

Differences. Good and bad.

What's normal … unhinged?

She fiddles with split ends.

Moans of pleasure.

Moans of despair.

Psychos.

Heroes.

She often feels her mind is folding in on itself. (Don't say origami.) She is an artist. Or at least she sings. (For now.)

Her heart beats: music, men. She moans *for* and *because of* each.

She's not stupid. She's just looking for something. The search may be enough. Maiko's moans are *of* everything and her moans are *for* them all.

She must mean something moan about something mean something moan about something mean something moan about something she is human one of the humans so close to these woods and all that is about to happen there ...

On a road.

Heading.

Hot as hell.

A house awaits.

3

Jason drives.

His muscular, tattooed arms out in front of him. Ropey arms. Thick veins. Soft blonde hairs when the light catches. He's smoking a joint at the same time and flicking ash out the open window. The air-con doesn't work in the van – they got it cheap – so the windows are open wide and letting Can and their Japanese singer and marijuana ash out into the country's oppressive air.

He passes the joint to Maiko and she gladly takes and gladly tokes. If a police officer ever caught them with this stuff they'd be screwed for sure. Things might be looser in her bandmates' countries, but not around here. Everything is strict. But Maiko likes the idea of being caught – what could be more rock 'n' roll, what could be more punk? No one would bail her out. She left her family ages ago. They hardly even noticed she was gone (*Elon Musk's money, go back to him take it Grimes, girl, take it, take it*) were too busy with their jobs and their jobs and their jobs. They have nothing else. The Japanese: they work. Maiko doesn't. She's a singer. With these dickheads – *dickheads* is one word and not two, she discovered, it could also be the name of their band: The Dickheads. Ladies and gentlemen will you please welcome to the stage, The Dickheads. There's probably one already called that, in some lonely abandoned warehouse or in some patient dad's garage. Practising like crazy. Going nowhere fast.

So many bad names. Hard to settle on one. Hard to settle on anything. To settle down. *Band* suggests togetherness. Solidarity.

That is not the vibe they give off. What kind of vibe *do* they give off? Something awry. Something wrong. If it all does not come out in the wash it'll come out in a song.

Oppressive air.

Layers.

Maiko doesn't moan about the air or its oppressiveness, or at least not all that much. She's used to it. The others aren't. They complain all the time. The heat. The humidity. The lay of the land. The little bitches.

In the back of the van is Pete Illtyd, thirty-five years old, short, stocky, pale-faced with a gloomy demeanour – Maiko passes the joint back to him.

Jason is all: "Careful, don't set all our priceless analogue equipment on fire. Genki will never spring for new stuff."

Sarcastic.

Or is it *irony*?

In Japanese there is no difference; hardly any need for such. Who would ever speak in such a way?

Whatever.

Maiko doesn't think it's all that funny, whatever Jason or Pete say.

Genki is their manager: they'll have lots to say about him.

And what a name! Genki! Meaning: *cheerful;* meaning: *robust*. A healthy kind of name. Heart of gold. But business acumen … ?

Pete takes a drag of what he calls a *funny fag*.

Fag means something else where Jason's from, or at least it used to. That one got outlawed too. Cancelled. No one says *fag* anymore for gay men.

"I want to drive," says Pete.

"No, you're the shortest. My legs can't fit back there. It's like being on a fucking airplane. Coach."

Maiko giggles when Jason says things like that. She sometimes does this. Not often. But sometimes she does, she giggles; even puts her hand up to cover her mouth like a high school girl, like every high-stockinged, knock-kneed, short-skirted cliché there is – which is of course the stereotype that stirs the soups in all their pots. Sailor uniforms. Feet turned in so much the big toes almost nuzzle each other. A glimpse of white panties if they bend over to drop their pink feather-topped pencils. They all – the stupid males – they lap up that shit (*lap up*: she learned that too, and a kitten *laps up* milk, and *pussy* can mean two different things … but men want only one of them). And she does it sometimes, she just gives it to them, the stereotype, gives *in* to them, it's pathetic, she knows this. But at least she knows.

Pete's blushing, the *short-legs* jibe clearly having stung. His face looks wrung. "Sorry, you can drive on the way back."

That, most likely, will never happen. But Jason does sound sincere in his apology. His *sorrys* are usually authentic. Maiko knows his sincerity, his nature, she's seen his face when he's in the throes, when the blood floods all to one intent and purpose, and the face he wears when it occurs. When all the fireworks go off. The little death. In life. Where Schopenhauer says, "the devil's laughter is heard" (Pete quoted this to her, showing off, like he knew stuff). It would look a lot like agony if it weren't pure ecstasy.

"One whole week away, Pete," says Maiko, long toes on the dash, even though the plastic is hot.

Everything is hot. Is that plastic? What are things made of?

"You're stuck with us for one whole week."

Jason pipes in with: "Our honeymoon".

He knows he kneads Pete's nerves.

Pete snorts contempt. Takes the bait. Can't help himself, he's snide before he even knows what's happening, it just comes over him, it takes very little.

Jason knows how to bait him. He even taught Maiko that word: *bait*. Told Maiko about fishing in Montana. Hooks. Flies. Worms.

Nets. Slippery things. He made a joke, said he could be called *Jason Baitman*.

But she didn't get it. She doesn't get a lot of their cultural references. *Who?* More explaining. American actor. *Ozark*. Sometimes she pretends to listen; sometimes she even pretends to care.

"This isn't supposed to be a holiday," says Pete.

The others say nothing to this, a silence like the beginning of a séance. As if something will appear.

"You can actually get married when this is all done."

"A honeymoon comes *after* a marriage."

Jason and Maiko exchange a look, rolling their eyes in synchronicity.

Pete, of course, catches it. Baited. Hooked.

The van goes over bumpy terrain and Pete struggles for balance. The ride in the back and the blatant comfort the other two are having in the front is sure to be galling him.

"This is my band, remember. I'm the oldest. The founding member."

Jason parrots, *member*, doing his best Butthead, and tries not to burst into laughter. A child. Older than Maiko. Must be what? Thirty now? Thirty! But a child.

Pete ignores and continues, and Maiko is the one who thought of the idea of renting the country house in the first place. They told her it wasn't really a *country house*, just a *house in the country*. She didn't get that distinction either. Language was slippery. Like the fish in Montana rivers apparently.

"Supposed to be laying down tracks for a new record."

Pete says *record*. A throwback. He's not that old, but still.

"But we will, fuck's sake, chill."

Jason imitates Pete then with *my band, my band*. Further galls.

"Jesus. If you're the oldest you certainly don't act like it."

Pete hands the remainder of the joint back to Maiko, who sucks on it, one last drag, her thin lips pursed tight, sucking, sucking, and she throws it, out the open window. Fuck it.

"There'd better be food in that house, I'm fucking famished," Jason's stomach growls as he says this, right on cue to illustrate; it is as loud as the old van's internal rumblings.

Maiko is nodding, taking in the word. *Famished.* She knows *famine.* Has heard that one. She is able to make connections. She learns. About language. About them.

"They said the kitchen would be fully stocked," says Pete, authoritative, or always wanting to be.

She is so fucking bored and wants the CD changed, let's it be known:

"I'm bored with this shit."

Maiko moans when she is bored. She used to piss off every teacher she ever had. No one moaned out of boredom in those old classes, they used to just put up with it. They were stoical. Put up. Shut up. That was a philosophy they all knew. They say it about her people all the time.

(Who?

Who says?

Jason.

Pete probably.

Her people?

The Japanese?)

Maiko moaned on those hard classroom seats. Her almost fleshless bottom. Bone on the hard wood, it fucking hurt. Chalk motes flying from the board proposing universes.

Board.

Bored.

Homophones.

She moaned.

Life could be a whole lot better.

But it isn't.

Then she ended up with her bandmates. Dickheads. How do you get from a boring classroom to a beat-up old van on a day that might be the hottest on record?
You just do.

4

The house says: I have no need to devour you, you will probably devour yourselves.

5

Maiko groans having to take her long toes off the sun-hot dash, and she rummages around for a CD from the glove box stash. She changes the music to lighter, poppier stuff: vocoders, shiny synths, lifting choruses.

"That's not the kind of music we'll be aiming for, I hope you know that," says Pete, ever the minor key. In the ointment, the flea.

"We haven't even arrived and already you're giving us shit," Jason, blunt.

Maiko scratches at her face: sweat? A bug? She can't tell.

Something suddenly darts out across the road in front of the van, alarming them, fully frightening.

Jason swerves but manages to keep the vehicle steady, on course.

Pete crashes in the back against the equipment, banging his head, which serves only to irritate him further.

"Fuck's sake!"

"Sorry. Something ran out. Close call."

Maiko looks a little rattled, pulling her mass of hair-mess from her thin face and settles her feet on the dirty floor of the dirty van, slips her flip-flops back on.

"What was it?"

Pete is righting himself in the back, trying not to look aggrieved, "Fuck knows, a raccoon dog or something."

Maiko disagrees with the American, "I've never seen a raccoon dog move that fast."

"And you'd know, *inakamono*," says Jason.

Pete doesn't get it, and Jason is happy to explicate: it means *country bumpkin.*

"You'll have to brush up on your Japanese, Peter. How long you've been here now?"

Jibes.

Ribs.

Gentle pokes.

Often … not so gentle.

Pete gives him a withering look in the mirror.

Jason pulls one of his smiles, happy for Pete to catch it.

Unsatisfied as yet, Jason decides to goad that little bit further, "What were you before you became a musician? Back in Wales, I mean. A botany student, right? Expert on plants and shit."

Maiko is listening intently: it is way better than the frivolous pop that's playing, has more undercurrents, or is that *overtones*? Arguments like this are riveting for her, and all so frequent these days. Are all bands like this? Are all families? *Band* suggests solidarity. *Family* too. How wrong everyone is. How completely wrong.

"Doesn't matter about my past. And I'm not here to chat with the locals in Japanese, am I, mate? I'm here to make fucking music."

"Fucking music. You're right. Music to fuck to. You're such an artist."

Maiko doesn't snigger this time. She's not taking sides on this one. Knows better. They can have at it. These mere children. It's too hot for this kind of bullshit.

A hobo, dressed in cruddy, mud-caked clothes, appears, out of the blue. He could be from a dream, from a grainy old VHS TV drama someone hadn't taped over, could be even …

But no, he's real enough, walking along the road slowly towards them, all weary tread, moribund, a bowed head, bandy legs, near broken from the weight of the world, gravity, the heat of the hellish noon.

"Check out the state of this poor fucker. What are you slowing down for?" Maiko wants faster.

The house.

A shower.

End of grime.

End this stifling time.

"Directions," says Jason.

"I know where we're going, Jay."

Sometimes she sounds so confident. With a microphone she's like that. Like you can utterly trust her. Like she means what she says, or means what she sings, or those little moans she gives out between lines, containing so much world-weariness – from one so young! – or full of philosophical enquiry, but really, really just moans from the pit of herself.

Lines?

Lines of what?

"Well … I kinda know where we are going."

And sometimes she doesn't sound so confident at all. Sometimes sounds lost. A measly mewl from the runt of the litter, forgotten, as mama abandons the den, and who knows what is going to stick in its paw and scoop you out.

"Anyway, it's on the phone."

"Phones aren't working up here, sweetheart. Check your signal."

Maiko does. Jason's right. Useless. Like this place was only ever *needed* for VHS and fuzzy footage, or hasn't moved on from that era yet. This place might never move on. A land forgotten, that knows no progress. Things get trapped here.

Pete now has his head between the front two and he's panicked. He's spotted the approaching hobo and he's all a-fluster, "No! Don't stop! Keep going! Go!"

Jason ignores, slows even more, anything to spite. He pulls the van right up near the hirsute walking man, this devil of dishevelment, this darling of the dust. Wild eyes of him, this hobo, they shine as if he's about to be saved, or as if he's found the light (no devil then) – and there's plenty of that to go around: light, the sun, sterner than ever, landing rays on every static thing, every moving thing too; things moving languorously about the day, half wishing they were dead, enough is enough, quite enough, cracking open the rocks, its intensity, heat, this heat, and the wetness too, forever encroaching, humidity – how can they co-exist with such ferocity, the heat, the wetness, enclosing, it seems to seep into the very spaces between atoms.

Maiko rolls down her window fully when close to the filthy man – odours almost taking tangible form, like ectoplasm. He's all smiles though, knows not that he stinks perhaps, knows not that he suffuses the air and further swells the stuffiness with his own putridity, shows no awareness, or no embarrassment, and is about to speak when Jason Kiberd, American, brought up on road movies and the getaway cars of gritty grifters, puts his foot down and speeds off, away, away, more dust for the mess of a man who must stand and be cloaked in it, just left to choke on it.

Pete is sent crashing about in the back of the van again. Hurt from hard amps on his body, metal stands, fulsome things, and bruising.

But it is Maiko who curses the driving, the driver, "Jason! Jesus, what the…"

She has learned to swear with *Jesus*. Has learned *fucks* and *bitches* – they are all expelled with such ease now, they come so naturally to her.

"Sorry, the smell was too much," says the driver.

"He could have told us where to go."

"We'll figure it out, sweetheart."

The *sweetheart* is for Maiko. But of course, really, it is for Pete.

They drive, dishing up dust and dust and dust and Pete readjusts himself in the back, is annoyed again, by everything, by himself, by everything.

A thought strikes Jason, like thoughts do, and often songs and lyrics and melodies, too.

"Don't you think he looked a lot like Genki?"

Maiko's split ends, such a concern (not hobos or humidity), her long fingers toying with strands, her eyes focused on the minute damage, everything, even the smallest gets ripped apart, you only have to look carefully, to notice these things, she's only half listening.

"That old tramp? Yeah. I guess," she says. "Like … if you shaved him, washed him. You'd need a hose to get that amount of dirt off him."

"Sure. And that suit he had on. Probably worth something. Once upon a time. How is he even wearing it? This heat. This fucking humidity."

Jason uses *fucking* too much. Jason wants to fuck too much.

Pete is avoiding all this. Takes no part in their conversation. He's watching Maiko lighting up a cigarette (he's less nervous now) and watching her relaxed position. How quickly she acclimatizes to everything. Toes on the dash again. How long they are. Digits. What a funny word. Numbers. And fingers and toes! In Japanese he knows the same word is used for fingers *and* toes. No difference. *Yubi.* See, he does know stuff, he has learned. They have all learned and they will have more to learn, about things, about each other, about this road they are on. The dust rising from it. The hot sun bearing down upon it. What a world they are in. Stifling. There's no end to it. When they think it's all over, that things couldn't possibly get any worse, it just trundles on, and then it does get worse, hotter, it gets much much worse. But yes, less nervous now.

"Shake the dust off your feet."

In unison, Maiko and Jason: "What?"

"Nothing. Bible. Lines remembered."

Eye-rolling from his bandmates. This day is already too long.

Pete, more at home now, is watching the way she moves. He leans forward, his head between them again, coming between them, yes, coming between them, less nervous, as if something has been elided, something passed.

"You promised you wouldn't smoke so much, your voice," Pete needles.

Pete has the prickles of a porcupine.

Maiko and Jason deliberately ignore. Different wavelengths.

"Wonder where he was going, that poor old dude," Jason muses.

"Forget about him. Keep going." This from the head in the middle. The other two, the front two, have such beautiful bodies. Not him. Not the one with his head in the middle. Pete. In the back of the van. Relegated. The leader. Relegated. This could irk.

Maiko is not from around here but she is hazarding a guess. A country girl, sure, but not this part of the country. Aren't all country places the same? Trees, farms, dirt roads, dry mud or mulch, depending on the season, insects, animals, night owls and indiscernible howls, men and women with broken teeth, far from dentists, or too far gone to even care, an asparagus-y pissy stench about all of them; things grown, by themselves, consumed by (with) themselves.

They drive a little further down the road until they see an old wooden arrow sign pointing right. A sign. The shape of an arrow. Something obviously crafted. Things couldn't be clearer.

"That's the one! Where Genki said it would be," Maiko, a sudden joy in her voice, the promise of a shower, a toilet to sit on and not behind a bush with wet ravines forming around her feet.

Pete is looking shifty (the mention of their manager), he's shifting uncomfortably in the back again; he does not like looking so small among all the larger, worthier, useful equipment, those functional things, clear in purpose, if wired properly. Is Pete wired properly? His moods change so often, like the weather back home – not here. Here it stays the same. Long stretches of it. Fucking hot. Could drive a soul insane. He's trapped in all that. Trapped.

And they are still in the van.

And still he's in the back of it.

Not front where he has every right to be: band leader, front and centre.

"He's not going to be joining us though, is he? Hardly going to leave Roppongi Hills for us … Genki … is he?" says Pete.

They ignore, as they've done before, it's easier, his tetchiness, Pete's sores. Pete's a bore.

Jason turns the van in the direction the arrow woodenly points, and they begin a climb on a steep incline through dense woodland, out of the shine.

"No one wants to hear the kind of music we play," says Maiko, apropos of nothing.

"That's why we're here. Everything's going to change."

"He's right. Old Petey boy. That's why he be the leader of this here band," Jason laughs, his preposterous honky-tonk hokum, but then he grows grave, as the woodland throws upon them even greater shade. "Seriously though, we are gonna change."

He then begins to tell of an article he read online recently, an interview with the Pet Shop Boys.

"Who?"

"Doesn't matter. Old pop queens. But the singer said that the acoustic guitar should be banned. He kinda had a point, don't you think?"

Pete and Maiko nod.

"Anyway, Genki will land us a good deal. We'll cut the record when we get back to the city." Jason says *record* too, from a different g-g-generation. "Tour later in the year. Things are going to start looking up. A breeze."

Maiko smiles at him, his positivity infectious.

Pete views both of them in the mirror, sceptically, jealously, his eyes narrow as if plotting, as they drive deeper into the woods, deeper, nature, deeper into the woods, deeper.

Maiko's name means "dance child". She likes this. Something her parents did actually get right. People ask her if her name has anything to do with the maiko of Kyoto, those apprentice geisha whose job it is to enliven the banquet by singing and dancing in Gion. She tells them yes; she was conceived while her parents had holidayed in Kyoto – how they had managed to get some time off she never investigated. She does not add that this makes her happy because it was perhaps one of the only times her parents proved that they actually loved each other, and had expressed it, for however short that while. And it all led to her being here. Hurrah.

Dance child.

Are names somehow prophetic? What happens to be bestowed upon one … or do you just get lucky with a name sometimes? She doesn't know yet the concept of nominative determinism.

Pete said his family name was Welsh and meant "multitude of land."

Jason said he never knew, and never checked, but a grandfather was Irish, so maybe … but he said he never really cared. He did name his cock "the slayer", and said that every man names his cock, and Maiko nearly gagged – not on the cock, but on the stupidity. He tried to brush it off, saying it was the name of a heavy rock outfit in the 80s, Slayer, which didn't help her any; she still took it in her hand that time and had to restrain herself from biting it off. Some French philosopher had said – she'd read, months previous, online again – that all men must spend their time restraining themselves. And how much it took to achieve this. The philosopher said nothing about women.

Maiko could.

Bite it off, she means.

She could, really.

Restrain herself?

Or just have a right moan about the injustice of everything.

Or the stupidity.

6

The house says: I am not a squatting frog. Have some bloody respect for where you are and what you deal with.

7

They pull up in front of the house and they pile out of the van, stretching limbs, yawning.

"So, this is it! Magnificent, eh?"

Maiko gets that this is Jason's sarcasm, so she tries to sound sensible, "It's what we need. Solitude. No interruptions."

"Not exactly Nellcôte though, is it Pete?"

"What's Nellcôte?"

Pete explains to her that it was the French mansion where The Rolling Stones recorded *Exile on Main Street*. Maiko, clueless again, wonders why she even bothers. The dickheads.

"It'll do." She says this to save face. And she tells them that the sooner they get down to making music, the happier they will all be. The words ring hollow, but she had to say something, it's a sort of pep, a rallying.

Doubt lingers; for all three of them. They are full of doubt, doubting themselves, doubting one another, it will be so hard for them to lose that feeling.

She tries another line. Different tack.

"You two should start acting like friends again. I don't know why we have to have all this tension all the time."

Pete stares at Jason.

Jason doesn't respond.

Leaves and branches react to a small wind, but it's so slight, hardly enough to dry the sweat off the musicians' faces. Sweat is still a glaze upon them.

Jason sniffs the air, reminding himself of the old family dog that used to run the open Montana spaces, the length and breadth of it, bounding, boundless energy. But the dog … the dog is long dead.

"Does this place smell a bit weird to you? Like … *off?*"

He recalls the trudging tramp, that hobo they encountered, the nauseating stench; perhaps some of that has remained, molecules having jumped from him to them, lingering there in their scant attire, or on their very skin. Gross.

The others shrug.

"You're just not used to *this* countryside; different from the countryside of North America," Maiko says.

"Perhaps you're right. We are aliens here."

They begin to load the equipment into the house. Heavy are the things they haul, their lives, stories, faults in their bones, so young and yet so torn, their toil, hot blood from the heat's severity, blood that's almost a-boil, heavy loads, speakers, things that will only amplify their voices, adding to their problems, adding only more weight, dragging them, dragging the stuff inside, flagging, under the weight, under the weight of things, this is their world.

Maiko stops for a moment when she thinks she hears something moving in the bushes. She looks around, her head raised in alertness, pert, a meerkat in a skirt. When she hears nothing further (just wind again, a slight leave-rustle) she carries on with her, *their* work.

Inside.

Main room.

In the white room, with black curtains, they are stationed.

Equipment all around them, surrounding. They are taking in their new environment, getting acquainted – none of them look particularly enamoured, three faces glum, but this is nothing new for them, rarely are they impressed, they have to dig deep to find something that will bring them cheer.

Before he begins his snoop around the place, Jason ridiculously rants. He rants on about haunted mansions and Scooby Doo and the Mystery Machine, just like the van they were in, he says, and a dog eating a tower of hamburgers with his stoner friend, and how the villain that is unmasked at the end is always so completely predictable. It was always going to be either him or his wife, there were hardly any other characters in it for fuck's sake! Except the jolly four and their big brown dog. One of the girls was sexy, kind of orange hair, skinny, slender hand on hip, the other was deliberately not, heavy sweaters and massive glasses, it was so cruel, the writers simply had to be male.

Maiko has no idea what Jason is talking about.

Dogs?

Towers of hamburgers?

And then he ends his mystifying spiel still laughing to himself and saying that he is going to go and *see where the bodies are buried.*

Maiko doesn't get that joke either.

Jason opens the refrigerator, thrilled to see that he has not been lied to – it is stocked full. He takes out a can of beer and cracks it open, drinks, burps, and sated he sighs.

Pete checks the bathroom, checks to see if the taps and shower are working. They are. Water flows, a little brown at first but soon clearing. He decides to take a piss while he is there. A horsey stream. The build-up of the van: cramped space and no relief. But liberation now; sated, he sighs, too.

Maiko ambles up the stairs, a few boards creaking under her bare feet and she goes to nose around all three bedrooms. There are no beds, instead: futons stacked in the corner of each, she seems pleased enough. No roaches scurry. Not like her boxy apartment in Tokyo. Those livewire, hard-shelled (hard as nails) bugs always conspiring under her refrigerator, their frantic mini-rattles across the floor in the dead of night when the lights are off, which gives them licence.

She goes to a window, opens it to let the air in and to let the musty ghosts out. She's not superstitious, but she can never be too careful. She grew up in rural areas like this, and the people, her people (*her* people?), believed in the spirits inside everything, stemmed from old religions, old acceptances, nature being deeper than even the best microscopes could manage to show. But let the good air in anyway. It will cool the rooms, if a wind is to be kind enough to come and assuage the clammy clasp of the place.

She allows herself a moment to gaze out and survey the scene. For a split second she thinks she spots a shape in the nearby woods, some shadow lurking there. The sun is in her eyes and she squints, trying to focus – but whatever it is has gone. A serow could've scarpered. Or a wild boar has barged away for a forest forage elsewhere.

She knows herself to be an animal that also needs. She will need something. Will need something or other. Food or shelter. Or no, not those. The thrust of sex, yes. Probably that, to sate her. But it passes, this brief caprice.

She goes about setting up one of the futons on the *tatami* floor. When it's done she lies on it, stretching out her long, lithe body as much as she can. She had done rhythmic gymnastics in school, and her flexibility is still there, in the yoga poses she adopts whenever she has time or notion. It feels good, the body reacting, the body reaching, the limbs testing outer limits, hitting spaces that seem beyond her … but she gets there. Her will. Determination. And with it comes the deep breathing, and the consequential relaxation, a tuning fork easing down into its lesser, softer vibrations, softer frequencies … almost as if she is home.

Maiko once made a woman moan, and she moaned along in tandem.

No, not a *woman*, a *girl*. They were not yet women. A *girl*. For they were young and barely out of high school, barely knew which end was which. All innocent. But all eager. Keen for experimentation and a lurch for a greater understanding of the world they inhabited. Keen.

Sayuri had come to her house, some pretext, a game, or just hanging out – it's so long ago now that Maiko cannot remember the reasons, or the exact year, or even which season. But she remembers the feeling of the day, the vibrations in the bedroom, as if the air had been electrically charged. They had spent time looking at scrapbooks, photo albums, anything to get two bodies closer together and focused on one thing, eyes trained on a fixed item, the same direction. It only took for one of them to break that fix and glance at the other to get them both started, not a word, not a single word was necessary; a gulp perhaps, a dry swallowing: that was the only sound, hardly interrupting. And soon they were off and fondling. Soon they were entering private spaces, releasing private moans that weren't private anymore but…shared; yes, a sense of sharing everything, the room, the day, the play.

What Maiko remembers most is how plain the girl was, yet how much effort she had put in to surmount all that. She hadn't much to go on. Her head seemed too big for her body, her shoulders too rounded, as if she shied of her own being and was forever pulling inward on herself; her feet turned in, the right more than the left – how she even managed to support her own skinny frame and that large head was something of a mystery; she looked as if she was on strings and controlled by a puppet master, loose and floppy, and seemed always about to collapse in a heap should those life-strings get cut. Small dark brown, almost-black dots or moles, which she called *beauty spots,* were scattered all over her face and body, and Maiko tried to touch each one of them, counting, accounting for them, wondering why such things existed in the first place – a flaw in the makeup, or just something to focus on, and the thin-limbed slip of a thing duly moaned under the curious touch of her tips.

She made such an effort that girl, such an effort to please and be pleased, her thick lips moue-d to be kissed.

So little to go on. So little. No beauty. But her eyes were made up and they shone. And her hair glistened. And her cheeks blushed with the perfect amount of rouge – someone must have taught her how, so expert was her glow. And the small breasts, with puffy nipples that seemed too large, too showy to be there, rings for attention, they hardened to it, hardened to the slightest attention. Standing. Erect.

Maiko moans to the memory.

She would have that girl all over again if she could, any season, without any reason. Sayuri. That was what she went by. The first part of her name meant *thread* or *silk*, and that was what Maiko could feel, and feels it still, something smooth, as if there were no problems in the world that day, certainly no horror, and it was thus worth recalling; it could be savoured at any time; and *thread* meant connection. Connection. Connection. Though *thread* was also thin and feeble, and just as easily as it could be savoured, it could be severed.

8

The house says: there are things buried.
But some things do not remain so.
Some things want to crawl back out from where you've stuffed them.

9

Pete stands with his hands on his hips.

"This is where we will set up. Obviously. The biggest space."

Their headquarters for the foreseeable future, this large white room, black curtains to block out the searing sun – a good idea, whoever thought of that.

"Sure thing ... *boss*." Jason, of course.

Maiko doesn't have the nerve yet to attempt such a jibe. All three of them, all awkward. They have known each other for some time, but you'd never guess, sometimes so nervous of each other, suspicious. Shuffling on the old carpet, wearing its worn fibres even further.

"Let's unpack all the equipment."

Jason, defiant, childishly so, wants to rebel against his *boss's* instructions; he goes to the sofa and plops down in a great show of laziness, raising his feet on the low coffee table, and smiling foolishly at the frowning band leader.

Maiko seems to be in agreement with her boyfriend, and faces Pete.

"Not today ... surely?"

"Why not?"

"Because we just got here."

"We need time to ... settle."

Jason raises his beer to salute the idea.

Pete looks immediately annoyed at the mutiny, but he realizes he has no other choice in the matter. This is not how he wants to begin events. This is not the way his orders should be … just downright *disobeyed* like that. His father, his father had orders and they were never disobeyed. Lest the lash. His family had …

"We'll play tomorrow dude, early. Seriously. When the cock crows."

Jason drinks from his beer until Maiko snatches it right out of his hand and takes a deep and satisfying drink herself. It's cooler inside this dark house, but not all that much.

"There are plenty in the fridge. And more out back in the storage room."

Maiko beams at this good news, she could do with letting go, and there was such a thirst on her now, such a tormenting thirst, the day they've had, the travel.

She wants to know about their other *stimulants* too. For the letting go. For the prospect of fun. There had to be some. There had to be some fun in all of this. If not … what was the point of them coming here?

"So … you did bring the magic box, yeah?"

"Do you think I'd forget the most important thing?"

Jason rises from the couch then, and smiling idiotically, begins singing idiotically: *The magic box, the magic box …* He continues this puerile refrain as he rummages through his stuff, and eventually finds what he is looking for: a grey cash box, the kind that needs a key to unlock.

The key hangs from his neck on a silver chain and he pulls it out from under his sweaty Ramones T-shirt and holds it up as if it is a religious relic, as if it were the key to unlock all things. The mysteries of the universe. The answer to all the big questions. All his movements are exaggerated – he is not even drunk yet, but clearly it is all just to annoy *Boss* Pete; it never takes much, and he succeeds yet again.

Maiko girlishly giggles as Jason opens the box with an ostentatious flourish.

"Voilà!"

"Nice."

The American runs his fingers through his collection of drugs. He closes his eyes and ostentatiously, exaggerating again, lets his fingers caress the goods, contemplating possibilities – that's what the box holds for him: possibilities.

"Everything you could wish for," he says. "Pills. Thrills."

"Bellyaches," says Pete.

"What?"

Maiko doesn't get Pete's reference; it must be another foreign rock music reference. Won't be the last time. This confusion.

"Nothing. A Happy Mondays record, back in the day … never mind."

Jason switches his attention to something that's been bothering him for hours now.

"Food first, man. I gotta eat something. It's been crazy long."

He grabs Maiko by the wrists and tries to drag her off to the kitchen, but she's having none of it.

"Fuck off! Make your own stuff."

Jason groans and heads to the kitchen, the box of drugs left open like a mini pirate's chest in the middle of the floor; no gold sovereigns, no shining jewels, but equally precious the things inside – resplendent they were in their own way, in their capacity.

Pete and Maiko are left with nowhere else to look but at it, the box, the centrepiece to a salacious banquet.

Maiko remembers Sayuri, the girl from her youth, how they had stared at the scrapbook in front of them, waiting for the first move to be made. Such tension then. An apiary in her stomach. But the buzz had been so magnificent.

She looks at Pete, "Are you OK?"

"Why wouldn't I be?"

"Ever since I joined the group you've become … I don't know … more … *reserved*."

It was Genki's idea to add a lead singer. To add a *female*. They lacked *sex-appeal* on their own. They lacked a focal point. They lacked presence. They had the skills all right, the musical know-how, had even that closeness, that understanding that comes from seemingly fraternal musicians playing so well in harmony – they had all that in spades, but still: a *lack*.

Genki, the go-getter, knew of Maiko, and knew that she sang well from open mic sets and karaoke parties. She was attractive enough to draw people in, had a certain magnetism, a certain sway when she graced the stage, and the way her hair hung over her face, boys and girls had to wait patiently for it to part and get a flash of white teeth (white light, white heat). The men acquiesced. Jason was prepared to give it a go. Pete, through frowns, through scowls, through harrumphs, eventually agreed to the proposal, too.

Pete doesn't reply now. His eyes are still on the box. It's like Maiko is not even there. A wraith ignored. It's something she can moan about later.

"Look, I know it was just you two for so long, but really, the last EP was good. The album will be even better."

The EP was an online-only release. Nothing physical. Few downloads. Pete doesn't even want to think about it. He never wants to think of failure. What would his uncle have said to that – *it should not even cross your mind!* He maintains his moody silence.

"You like my voice, don't you?"

He nods shyly, a schoolchild being suddenly cajoled by someone older, a nurse or a carer say, someone clearly more mature, and softer, and clearly more beautiful.

"Well then?"

She gives him time but still he will not speak.

"Or is this a case of Yoko coming to break up the band? Isn't that your thing? Mentioning foreign bands from the past knowing that I have no idea what you're talking about. A way of keeping me out of the loop. Well, I have heard of Ono Yoko. Japanese … after all. So, she's bound to get the blame."

Loop.

Bound to.

After all.

The phrases she acquires.

"Look, I just want everything to go according to plan. No fuck-ups," he says, finally.

She almost reaches out to hold his hand.

But she holds back.

"It'll be fine. We've got no distractions out here."

Pete points to the drugs, "I told him to leave those behind."

"They're just for a little ... recreational use. Fun Time."

It was the name of a record Pete played endlessly. The Stooges. But she doesn't bring that up now.

Pete pouts.

Things are not going his way.

Control.

Leadership.

His eyes are narrow, disapproving.

"Don't look at me like that, Pete. I've seen you smoke enough weed. And other little bumps, too."

Weed.

Bumps.

Jargon she uses now. Jargon from Jason. You must listen in, you must pay attention. The drugs too, from Jason, pushed. Once she was an innocent: in a dusty classroom, motes on sunbeams before the curtain got pulled across and darkness fell on fawny faces; but things change, dust gets carried on air-currents all the time, there is no saying as to where it all goes, where it will land, it just gets carried along.

She remembers one night, a live event, some dingy rock venue, some dingy toilet. Pete was inside with another rock fan, younger than him, some skinny coked-up skeleton, pupils large and busy hands. The door of the toilet was open; anyone could see in and no one cared. Maiko was outside, talking to a punkish girl, equally coked, all black lips, spiky hair, all piercings, black demeanour: a stance. Maiko could see the open toilet stall in the men's, Pete emptying some white powder onto a side ledge and bending to it and snorting the line with a rolled-up banknote like he'd been doing it all his life. He became jollier instantaneously, something she has not seen since.

Pete passed right by Maiko and the punk that night, fizzing with energy. Maiko grabbed him by the arm and dragged him close, wiping away the white remnant that was evident under his nose. He smiled at her in gratitude – he didn't even know her then – and he continued on his way in the direction of the music, the skeleton boy in tow, trying to grapple him from behind.

Maiko pats the vacant space of the sofa.

A gesture.

Peace.

Be still with me.

You're safe.

No one here will hurt you.

"C'mon. Sit. Loosen up."

Pete obliges – his schoolboy-look still not dissipated, his hooded eyes, forlorn – obliges, yes … but still he keeps his distance.

"I know you're fond of a little mushroom every now and again, am I right?"

Pete nods towards the box.

"There are none in there."

"Pete, you're in the fucking countryside. There are loads of things growing out there. Isn't that your specialty? I mean … in the past. What's the word?"

"Botany."

"Yeah, *botany.*"

Pete still can't manage to cast off his shawl of sullenness.

"Tell you what," she goes. "Why don't we go out looking for some tomorrow? Just the two of us. Let Jason set up the equipment, for a change."

She leans over and into him. She takes his face in her hands and plants an affectionate, sisterly kiss on his cheek.

Pete looks stunned, blushes uncomfortably, is not a little reviled; a siege of unheralded emotions upon him, but nowhere to hide.

"There. Friends?"

"Suppose."

She gets off the sofa and goes to the kitchen. He watches the sway of her hips in her light summer skirt as she moves away. He touches the cheek where she had laid a kiss upon him, but his expression is now blank, or shows only a sort of puzzlement: unfathomable humans, and the things they do.

Pete sits for a few minutes humming hauntingly to himself. His brow is furrowed, deep in deliberation. He shakes himself out of it and goes to the littered cases of equipment. He pulls out an acoustic guitar and begins tuning it.

"Fuck the Pet Shop Boys."

There is no one to hear this proclamation.

When satisfied he's got the instrument in tune he starts to strum, gently, humming again.

Suddenly Jason is there, standing at the door, watching him. Pete stops his strumming and looks at him directly, confrontationally. A silent standoff.

Jason begins to feel uncomfortable and shuffles on his feet. Maybe that's why the carpet has grown so worn, scores of feet-shufflers through the decades, all too afraid to actually deal with their dilemmas.

An almost otherworldly look comes over Pete, it's eerie – Jason has seen it before, and so he shuffles even more, knows what might come, what dangers could … if oxygen given, or if fuel added.

Pete strums again, then starts to sing, in a high-pitched, ugly whine.

The lyrics of the song tell of a guy called Jason undressing another guy, but while doing so he kept his boots on.

Pete stops.

Silence then.

The abruptness is alarming, as alarming as the slice of dirge that had been dished out.

Whatever the fuck that was.

Was that supposed to be a song?

A clock ticks in the corner.

It could contain a bomb.

Pete's look changes from otherworldly to semi-deranged, a contortion there, a morphing, and flashes of something sinister there in his eyes; Jason has seen this before too, this sudden turning, and the smile now, Pete's smile, it holds no mirth.

"Did you write that?"

"No."

"What is it?"

"It's a Perfume Genius song."

"What's it called?"

"'Jason'."

"Seriously?"

"Yes."

Jason glares severely, his ropey muscles twitch, tattoos move.

Another tense standoff: hardly blinking, either of them, hardly breathing.

The guitar sits like a swollen, neglected child in Pete's lap, parents too busy to give it the love it requires, in this, their moment of domestic duress.

Maiko then appears at Jason's shoulder. She has come to them and is eating something, hunger having gotten the better of her, too.

She shows no elegance in the open-mouthed-munch, bits of dried seaweed greening her teeth.

Not caring, cheerfully, she addresses the elder, "You writing already?"

"No."

"Never rests, does he?" says Jason. "Never lets things go."

Pete shrugs, sinister eyes softening and yielding to his customary gloom.

Maiko maintains her cheeriness, "We thought we'd have a barbecue. Jason found a grill and charcoal. We can cook outside. What do you think?"

"We don't have to ask his permission."

Pete nods as serenely as he can muster, looking no one in the eye.

"Go. Have your fun."

He starts strumming again.

They turn their backs on him.

Maiko once read a review on Pitchfork. The writer (Jenn Pelly, she loved the name) wrote of Angel Olsen (she loved that name, too): "She sings with the depth and candor of Patsy Cline, but her guitar chords are choppy, unpolished, underscoring the point: Life requires messes."

Life requires messes.

Life requires messes.

Maiko remembered how as a child she once daubed red paint across her dresses. She said to the mirror then that she wanted to be an artist and thought, even then, at that tender age, that this kind of action was requisite.

The paint was red, it looked like blood, which was, of course, the point.

Was there a point to art, and daubs, and fucking dumb Americans ... fucking *retreats* in the stifling countryside?

Her mother came back from work (her job her job her job) and found Maiko's messes, her destroyed dresses, and she wholeheartedly beat her, and she even tore one of them into strips (*tore strips off her*) and shoved them into Maiko's mouth.

Maiko gagged.

Couldn't moan.

Maiko could hardly breathe.
She thought for one terrifying second she would surely die.
She didn't.
She only fled.
Often, in fact … this fleeing.
Messes.
Memories of red paint.
Stains.
Maiko moans for the mess she often made of things. *Makes.*

10

The house says: you are not welcome here; the mat is just a lie, like everything else, it's just a lie.

11

Wafts.

The good smells.

Jason has long forgotten the putridity of the hirsute hobo. He's concentrating on the smell of the grilling food that lifts up to his face, making his tongue drench itself in anticipation.

Smoke: Jason sends smoke signals out to the world as if to say: we are human, us few here, and we are eating things that grow and things that were killed for us, we might even be eating you out there, you creatures out there in the forest. Us, eating you! That's just what we do.

Pete and Maiko are sitting on camping chairs and drinking from beer cans. They are far from the music they are supposed to be making. Needed time *to settle*. That was how she had put it.

"This shit smells so good, man. Genki, or whoever left all the food here, deserves serious praise, dude," says Jason. "This beef is quality. Look at that sizzle, man. C'mon bring over your plates."

He has grown loquacious in his drunkenness. Grown carefree and has indeed become settled. It hasn't taken long. It *is* like home. The home of woodland and camping with a fond father who showed him how to fish, how to cook what was caught, the sharp knife slicing, the bones extracted swiftly in one unit … before he died, before father … excruciating pain, the pancreas, fuck me, the worst of the lot … but he isn't going to mull on all that now, Jesus Christ, he's here to make music, but to eat first, to glutton it all up.

Pete and Maiko rise with their paper plates and Jason, deft with chopsticks, doles out sausages, slices of beef, onion, pumpkin.

The cook then sits to eat with them, joins the band, for they are that now, at least for this moment. Band.

And they all chew quietly for a few minutes, pensively gazing out at the surrounding woods, the mass of darkness – it appears like one block of black; *not* composed of the myriad things it really is.

"We're going to attract animals. The smells." Maiko is not sure who she is warning with this statement.

All three are unafraid. Even Pete, the city boy, as far as they are aware, is unafraid. Botany? How had he decided on such a thing? But he shows no signs of fear.

"They might be already surrounding us. Everything is hungry. Everything out to get you. When you least expect," says Pete, after a big glug on his beer.

Horror lines in a monotone … but no one bats an eyelid to whatever tactic he has in mind. They are too busy eating, drinking, eating, to care about campfire scares. The things out there, they are not human, but what can any of them do about any of that? What can they do, these mere humans? Cicadas and crickets, or are they katydids? Things that click and buzz and hum, like power lines, like amps just turned on. The odd thing fluttering among trees: birds, they suppose, as the creatures wing their way to roost and to repose. Pipistrelles picking every air pocket they blindly find. Pulsing things, instinct-driven, different kinds, things, things, things.

Jason farts, brings them back to the base and corporeal.

"Gross."

"It's OK sweetheart, we're in nature, gotta be natural. You're a fully-fledged member of the band now, gotta get used to our ways."

She does not know what that means: *fully-fledged*. It sounds like a mistake. It could be (the whole week could be a fucking mistake).

He's slurring too, Jason, acting like a dick. Yes, she's got to get used to their ways, sure. The Dickheads.

"*Your* ways," says Pete, wanting to be clear.

Pete always wants to be clear, unless he's mumbling something to himself, which he does more and more these days – they don't know who that's for, the mumbling, the muttering, voices in his head that he's trying to expunge perhaps, some kind of exorcism? The hope is that they are songs . . . and that they are songs that will work.

Good music.

Is that too much to ask for?

Is it?

They haven't even started.

The next day.

That's the plan.

Rise at the crack.

Or the cock's crow.

Now that they're actually in the countryside . . . yes the cock will crow.

Get down to it.

Work.

They'll see how that goes.

Work.

They'll see.

It's still muggy, it's still warm, no wind to dispel the smoke. Things indeed could be circling, hungry – what are these people inviting into their lives?

Smoke around their faces. Like in a pop video. But no one is dancing or moving or playing an instrument, they are merely sitting, silent and surly, eating, releasing methane.

"Right, seeing as the conversation is so fucking riveting . . . "

Pete is not mumbling now. He's crystal.

They look at him, neither hopeful nor despairing, knowing he'll persist, of course he will, the founding member.

"For the next album . . . if you were to suggest three words to describe how you'd want it to sound, what words would you use? Like . . . it can be anything. Noun. Verb. Whatever."

Pete sounds and looks authoritative, has taken advantage of the others' drunkenness to lord over them – they find this grating, but they are too far gone to really care right now, to put up any kind of fight.

They decide to comply, even if they can't quite yet think of the words their leader requires.

"Like if I said … *spacious … desert … cactus.*"

Jason's mind spins: Did he say *desert*? Wasn't *cactus* already the name of a Pixies song, and didn't David Bowie even cover it?

"Those aren't sounds, dude."

"Yeah, I know they aren't sounds, Jay. But they *suggest* sounds, like conceptually … you're not really getting this, are you?"

"Deep, man. You're so fucking deep."

"Just think, seriously. I want to know what we want. So we're all on the same page. I want an album with cohesion, unity. Not just a collection of songs. Something that … binds."

He gives them time to absorb what he is saying.

They only absorb more beer.

"No one does song collections anymore. There should be an underlying theme." He looks Jason straight in the eye; his next remark to be fully loaded, the point of a headhunter's dart laced with poison:

"Or words like … *betrayal.*"

Cicadas.

"Or … *false hope.*"

Crickets.

"Or … *lies.*"

Katydids.

A piece of charcoal crumbles into its companions in the embers and sparks fly before it begins its decay to ash.

Jason returns all this with a stern uncompromising look of his own, as if to say: *drop it, drop it, or I'll drop you.*

Maiko hasn't been fully tuned in. She's thinking her own thoughts, her neck craned up to look at the bounteous stars

– you never get the chance in the city and she misses this from her childhood. Her period is coming, any day now, and her body is moaning its imminence, nipples tender, hardening for no reason and purplier than usual. She drifts out of her spell and back to them.

"OK. I get the *spacious* thing. And instead of *desert* I'd say ... *natural* or *pure*."

She sips from her can before continuing.

"And maybe *rock*, but not like rock *music*, but like a rock formation, cliffs, or a guy carving something out of stone. Like a statue. Or someone breaking someone's head open ... with a rock."

"Jesus Christ!" Jason splutters beer all over himself.

"Sorry. Just some thoughts rattling around in my head."

"No, no, that's good Maiko, that's the kind of thing I had in mind when I posed ... "

Jason is the one to starting to tune out now. He's staring off into the trees, eyes glossing over. He's tired. Tipsy. Bored with the company. Chat only goes so far. There has to be action too. People get bored. People get bored if it's only endless discourse. Jason is, he's bored, wholly, he looks in the opposite direction.

Pete tries to reel him back in, "Jay, give us some words, mate."

Jason rises from his chair and goes to the grill, as much to stay awake as anything else. If he sits there any longer he'll just conk out – the heat from the grill and the smoke in his eyes and the long drive of the day and the boring conversation and the not-yet-sex which he doesn't want to be too tired for ... he wants to fuck her, the animal air has made that animal instinct stay alive ... he wants to fuck her, and hard, he shakes his limbs, almost as if he's limbering up for a fight.

"Yeah. I've got some words for you. A little song actually, it goes like this. *The magic box, the magic box* ... come along now folks, *the magic box, the magic box* ... "

He does a little dance, moronic again, with four eyes on him, which neither encourage nor remonstrate. Needs. He's full of them. He needs perking up. Needs stimulants. And kneads ... Pete's nerves. All this is so deliberate. Like when he's in a recording studio, at the desk: he knows what buttons to push.

The stupid dance continues.

Maiko does her high school girl giggle, an appreciation of his goofy talents. Or she just wants a fuck, too.

The beast roars inside Jason as he takes food from the barbecue and chows down on it, savagely.

Maiko could do with some stimulants now as well; something is also coming alive inside her, the beer no longer sufficient. Her period will be in a few days, definitely, woman, bound by the calendar, these men are clueless and can sail from month to month unfettered – she wants to get as much as she can before then.

"Where's the key?"

"In my pants. Come and get it."

Pete rolls his eyes. Here we go. A lapse into stupidity. His bandmates never that far away. Typical.

"No, seriously babe. The box is already open. Bring out some of those lovely little dissolve-ables."

Maiko does as she is told, rising with newfound vim … but obedient to him.

Pete looks on as if she stinks of nothing but sin. Lilith. *And the wild-cats shall meet with the jackals, and the satyr shall cry to his fellow; yea, the night-monster shall repose there, and shall find her a place of rest.*

"Should probably keep the box locked," says Jason. "Don't want any raccoon dogs stealing into the house at night and getting high on our stash."

He's delighted with that – a *tanuki* high on LSD; Jason laughs at his own creation.

Pete sits, brow-furrowed. He's not drunk, just immersed in his usual funk.

"Why do you have to act like such a fucking idiot?"

Jason still chews, ignores, sips from his can wildly, spills half over his chest and does not care. He's filthier than ever. Neither of them has washed, even though they all craved it on arrival. Hunger had gotten the better of them. And thirst. And now they reek like any tramp they're ever likely to meet.

"We're here for four or five days to do one simple thing, make music. And you're treating it like we're teenagers on our first trip away from Mommy and Daddy."

Jason stalls his silliness, his rage rising. He turns to face him, to face him down.

"If this is to do with…"

"With what?"

Cicadas.

Crickets.

Was that an owl?

Or a crow?

Crackle of dying coal.

"Nothing."

"No, go on, say it."

Katydids.

Crickets.

"She's part of the band now… and I fuck her… so what?"

Pete is shaking his head but Jason is not about to let this one go:

"If you're pissed because…"

"I'm not pissed, mate. I just want to put out some good music. There are bands back in the city that are a lot more adventurous than us, and making good tunes. And good money."

Jason flings the empty can aside. He wants to hear no more. But Pete persists.

"We're lost, Jay. I want us to be the best. At least better. Have you no pride anymore?"

Jason waves his hand dismissively, but he's reeled back in.

"You overthink. You always overthink things. It's just music, man. We'll do it."

Pete's hand begins to shake a little, a nervous reaction to all the nervous tension, and lines of scripture become alive inside him, memories of things learned, things forced upon him, from way back, way back.

The crickets seem to have gotten louder.

The cicadas or katydids or whatever they are, are also upping their noisy game.

Something squawks in the woods, some night fowl, it echoes around their heads. He looks to Jason. A plea now: "Just give it everything you've got, will you? For the sake of the band. Our future. Together."

"Sure. Just stop looking at us as if we've somehow betrayed you. It was Genki's idea to introduce a singer…"

He takes a long minute to consider his next words. His face has become tinged with sorrow, he is almost apologetic.

"What we did… you and I… together… I mean…"

The word *together.*

There it is again, echoing in the quiet country.

Pete has hope in his widening eyes: hope that his old friend will go on, give an explanation, it's due, some kind of repentance…

But Maiko interrupts the confession. She's got *treats* in her hand… and Pete's head hangs.

"Stick out your tongue."

She puts the tiniest, wafer-iest slip on her own tongue and then, saurian, slides it across Jason's ever-eager tongue, until the tab is surely there and already dissolving (like the band itself, unable to cope in the temperature, with the tempers, the humidity; dissolving, into the darkness of a place they do not know).

Jason's eyes stutter to a close, his long feminine lashes do a butterfly flutter-by and his mind sinks to a swirling that's a somewhere-else.

But somewhere else seems fine by him. Not here, not here near these acres of trees and a house that looks like a squatting frog.

There's a rustling in the woods.

Something moves out there.

It could be a wild boar, or a lost dog mad with starve-pangs, craven, craving... or larger yet, a deer, a bear.

Pete shows not the slightest unease. Perhaps he knows what might come, knows what might need to be... dealt with. Some things need finishing off, he thinks, especially if you don't do it right the first time.

The other two hear nothing. They are settling nicely into their trips. They've only taken a half each, a sharing, but it is enough to bend and wonderfully warp and make life out there (with Pete and Nothing) ... a bit more interesting.

Maiko goes to the portable CD player and presses play. Electronic dance music throbs up, pushes them into the pulsing rhythms of it. She begins to dance and Jason joins.

Crazy gyrating.

Close loins.

Soon they are grappling at one another, clawing hungrily, moaning as they do so, not caring where they are, or the *who* that is left to hear them.

The *who* that hears them, Pete, is watching on uselessly, nothing at all for him to do but drink from the can of beer that sits in the conveniently provided hole on the arm of his camping chair. His left hand trembles again. Bible lines flickering in his mind. Way, way back. Always like this in nervous moments, a falling back on ...

His mouth becomes a pinch of vindictiveness, plans begin to form, or have already been formed and are now reminding him – get on with it, get on with it.

He rises and walks a few feet towards the woods.

The others ignore him, nothing new there, easy to block out, they continue their course, their coarse courting, close; they stick out their tongues, saurian again, or forked? Are those horns that rise from their heads? The music is full and it's inside them.

Pete starts to talk aloud, to the woods, addressing. It is not the Bible this time. It's Kierkegaard. How can he remember such things?

Because they were drilled into him.

Only music can take these things away.

Drill.

Drown out.

Drill.

Drown out.

"Only the lower natures forget themselves and become something new. For instance, the butterfly has entirely forgotten that it was a caterpillar; perhaps in turn it can forget that it was a butterfly so completely that it can become a fish. The deeper natures never forget themselves and never become anything other than what they were."

Spinning Maiko stops spinning to pick up the last lines of Pete's crazed pontificating. She does not know why he addresses the trees, but she sees him on his knees and she says: "Deeper natures, yeah, deeper natures, yeah. It could be the name of a band. Why are you on your knees, Pete?"

It will not be the name of the band. Their new incarnation. What were they before? What were they even called? Who cares? Arbitrary. Dissolve. Right there, dissolving. The night is getting away from them. Two of them have to do something about it, before it's gone. They stagger away from the nightfeast and sway their way into the house.

The preacher, or at least the son of the preacher man, is left on his knees with the dark trees … and he spits on the ground in repulsion.

How can they just walk away from him?

He knew that was what would happen, knew it, but still and all …

How could Jason walk away from him?

Together was a word. *Together*, they knew.

He gets up and goes to the CD player, turns off its racket. Was it even music? He could create worlds much better than that. He will. He will be in control of everything. Just needs this night to pass. The next day should be a whole lot better. Deeper natures never forget themselves. He is only mumbling now, mumbling to himself, but he stops suddenly when he hears something rustling in the bushes.

He shows no signs of panic.

He is thoroughly composed.

He thinks he might even know what is there.

Who.

He thinks he knows *who* is there.

Gleeful laughs from inside the house distract him and he turns to these sounds. Up and down, he considers the house.

So, this is where they are to be contained.

Make something happen.

Make something happen Pete, for God's sake. God! His uncle had told him all about that. God. And nature. He studied nature. Botany. Plants and trees. Mush up those mushrooms into some tea and see what happens then. Philosophy. Ha. Right now he has only watery beer. What has Jason got in his hands right now? What does Maiko hold?

He turns once more to face the woods.

"Soon, my land, soon."

He feels the night begin to chill – it's only the lateness, the idea of things coming to end, not even the temperature, he decides to head back inside. He will hear them. He will hear what they do. Listen. When great music is about to be made … you need great ears to hear. To appreciate. You need to hear first. Hear it. Hear. Here we are now. Entertain us.

Sometimes when she is alone in her city bed she thinks about the moan of the universe. How it began like that, not with a bang. As if it was sorry for its own beginning, sorry for what it was about to do. It was more the moan of a child being dragged to kindergarten, not wanting any of it, not wanting to be responsible for the swirling things forming and growing. But it went along. It had been forced. By itself. By *the itself* it knew not of, and just did. No other choice in the matter … and the matter forming.

Thoughts in a lonely bed when there was no one on top of her, just the thoughts clambering on top of her, each one desiring attention.

She had left home. They were all too busy with other things. There was no real love. No one expected that kind of thing anymore. If ever they did. Not where she came from. People expected work from you, product, and then you keeled over. It was the only deal in town. But at least it was a deal. You got paid for it. You knew the rules, the parameters. What more did you want?

She once heard her parents. Her father moaning on top of her mother. Or was it her mother moaning from underneath. It didn't matter. The walls were thin. Hardly walls at all. Papery. Wafery. It was all over before she could even concentrate on it. It didn't matter. They had at least tried, she supposed. Some kind of effort to show love in a place where none ever really was. They had no time. Who ever had time? For love? What on earth are you talking about, girl? There's work the following day, work to be done. Her siblings never heard anything stirring at night. They probably never thought about the universe either, or wanted to make any kind of music. Their universe was hushed. Maiko's moaned.

Would it all end like that?

Would the universe end with a moan?

And what does it mean: to *sing*? What was she even doing?

Two men.

She plays with them.

She thought about this when she blew smoke out the window of her tiny city room in the middle of the huge night.

Or did they play with her?

Who toyed with whom?

It was so hard to come to grips with it all if you thought about it. Best be like her parents and not think about anything at all.

Put up.

Shut up.

One was on top of the other.

Who was on top of whom?

It didn't matter.

Some kind of deal had been brokered.

Thoughts in a lonely bed when there was no one on top of her, just the thoughts on top of her, just the clambering thoughts on top of her.

But right now. Jason. On top of her.

Pete is outside.

12

The house says: the next day things will *not* be a whole lot better. The house can moan more mightily than anything you've got to offer. Can crumple in on all of you ... if the house wants to.

What does the house want?

The same as anything else.

Peace.

Harmony.

The house is not getting what it wants.

13

Hectic in the discarding of clothes and for someone to be on top of her.

No thoughts that way. Just the physicality.

Inklings of thoughts slink off in slender-slides like worms through colander holes and sink somewhere unseen.

A pair.

All their movements are hurried and heated, desire always made manifest in a rush.

They both laugh when Jason stumbles on a pant leg and knocks his head against a closet door. Comedy: such a thing to break the scene, so unsolicited, breaks the momentum, they break momentarily from their roles.

But they are young and so they can soon resume, and are almost immediately back in their merry manic way, snatching at each other until every scant raiment has been pulled completely off: so simple an endeavour really, only needing a little concentration, a little conviction; and it is their realm now, and the dirt and the odours they had worried about are forgotten in the moment, and it's like no alternative could ever have possibly been on their minds: a single track they lay down, any embellishments, improvisations, will only serve to enhance.

But for all music ever being made … eventually a listener will be needed.

What good, what good music without the ears to hear?

Where is he?

Where is Pete?

Pete Illtyd is standing in the main room looking at all the cases of equipment strewn. His kingdom. Kingdom. Where he will be king (declare himself). And where he will make them sing. For him.

Quietly, he starts humming the second verse of the song he had sung for… sung *at* Jason. The song was even called "Jason". (Once they had grappled close *together* and the tumult of it… Jesus… Jason.) The words he burbles out now, emphasizing the lyrics, words like: *clumsily, shakily, afraid*. He shivers at the line about running *his hands up me*. Whose? Whose hands? The song is called "Jason" … nothing could ever be more apt.

In the bedroom the pair continues in their frenzied way, haphazard and high. Finally they are fully bare, knocking into each other, bone to bone, even kneecaps knock – sex's ever pacey quest soon to get started and soon get done; the gasps can be heard echoing around the room, echoing around the gaps of the house (unloved for so long), cobwebs almost set aquiver to ring like strings. Moonlight streams in as if it especially limns for them and skin is right and tight on skin.

Slowly, in contrast, downstairs, the singer has abandoned his pilfered tune and is removing his own clothes, almost ceremoniously.

He displays himself to the vacant room; nothing but their unpacked stuff (as yet unloved) to be his audience, but it has to be enough.

All his actions are actions of no-joy. When he sees himself reflected in the main window of the night he is as disconsolate as ever: receding hairline, waistline doing the opposite; so lacking, compared, always comparing himself to the others, to the now-pair, the beauties, inevitable, the comparing, the disappointment, they have height and they have pace and they have face and they have grace and they ooze it out all over the place. He silently bemoans his lack of presence and humours himself with the fact that he is the one with all the savagery, that all his power is based *on* savagery (bares his teeth to the night) and that when a great king of the past took notion to behead some treason-accused peasant: king did not baulk. Yes, a king can. A king can.

He smells blood from somewhere; maybe something has gotten trapped out there in the woods, in one of those hunters' traps. The terrible steel jaws always agape, a mechanism always hungry, always set, always non-discerning. Or maybe it's just his fancy. Either way he has become almost erect, growing ever in excitement, as the night beckons, requires. Prospects. The things he can do. Will do. The things he *will* do. His consolation is surely that he is creative. A king can.

Lust in the moonlit room.

Thrusts in the moonlit room.

Skin that glistens, smells and swells, and outside now, outside their door, a figure listens, ear-cocked.

"Wait."

"What?"

He doesn't want her to stop. The impatience of him, in it, the moment, the ever-drive, like the best *motorik* music, you cannot interrupt its rhythm. Why would you want to? Why would you ever want to stop until you're done? Get on with it.

"Can you hear something?"

They are stopped now, stalled ... and it is them who have their ears attuned.

Yes, definitely something, something is there, outside, listening in.

Something is close by.

Close.

They can sense another body.

But a threesome is only a threesome if all parties comply, otherwise violation, otherwise ... wrong.

They wait another minute and when the place, the whole squatting house, is totally still, they continue again, build up, the building up again, it doesn't take long, they are young and they can soon resume and are manic-merry again and it's all impetus and hot breath and hot sweat and the give and the take, the give and the take.

Outside the door: an animal. He is busy with himself. The sounds, the sounds, they are striving him on, no shame. His eyes are fixed on the blankness of the door. He can't see anything. He can see everything. The whole future, it's laid out before him. His consolation is that he is creative. Imagination. Or memory.

When their groans get louder and uncaring, when the moment can no longer be contained and they have no choice but to submit to the complete and necessary abandonment the occasion inevitably calls for ... the earth seems to shudder to a halt.

Outside he finishes, too. The human animal, crumpled, a heap. Is this the posture of a king? Spent. Such a lonely time he has spent.

Inside. No longer moaning. Maiko is wondering. Was that ... was that Pete outside and listening in on them? She had thought she had heard some shuffle, and a shadow under the gap in the door. She doesn't know whether to smile or to be afraid. She is not sure.

Jason is already half-snoring. It never takes long.

A threesome is only a threesome if all parties comply, otherwise violation, otherwise ...

She had a dream recently. She had been at some lakeside place, a place that seemed hot, like it was in Australia, some dry-heated land, not the wetness of the heat that swathes her now. In the dream, local, sun-kissed kids, surrounded her, pawed at her, and everyone treated her very well, fawning, almost in adoration, and she started to bond with them all, even speaking English in the dream, even mimicking their accents: it had all started out so well.

And then, typical dream-cut: a Cubist kitchen, and cooking meat with her father. Was that her father? Or some future lover? A husband? And the question arose: where had all the meat come from? She looked in the freezer and it was packed in transparent frosted film.

The man (it must have been her father) said he never wanted to leave the place, and maybe he'd actually bought the place, paid good money for the lakeside land, and that's why they were treating him so well. Like a lord.

And the meat. They kept eating loads of meat. Even in the dream, or while she slept, her actual body on the futon, she felt her stomach get tight and sore, like it had been too much (she had suffered from irritable bowel syndrome before, and this was it, come back to her, back to drive her crazy, her lower innards quivering from the stress of living, of thinking).

And children kept disappearing, day by day.

And children kept disappearing, day by day.

They brought the news to her every morning. Children were vanishing. Where had they gotten to? The little rascals, was it some kind of joke? But she was not laughing in the dream. No one was.

The end of the dream – after jump cuts, time-lurches – had her trying to escape the damned place. The realization had come upon her that the meat she had been eating *was* the children. She remembered seeing an eyeball in the freezer, frozen, looking up at her. And it had moved.

She'd fled.

And her father had watched her flee, wondering what the matter was. He never called after her, no instinct for protection. Did he even really know her name? It's Maiko. He just let her go.

The name of the town was Estival. She saw it on a sign as she ran away, barefoot and terrified, jagged stones cutting into her feet, the cries of babies on every street.

When she awoke from the dream she ran to her bathroom and threw up. She was sick for days after, some kind of stomach infection, something she had eaten perhaps, from a less than savoury noodle stall, or something rotten in some raw fish, untested, ingested. She couldn't be sure of the source.

Eyeball in the freezer.

She remembered the dream for a long time afterwards.

She couldn't be sure of the source.

14

A new day.
Promise?
Or equally shameful?

The door of Maiko's bedroom opens and bare-chested, boxer-shorted Jason Kiberd emerges, knuckling sleep-crust out of his adjusting eyes. In the morn-brightened musty room he leaves behind – a space that smells of bodies and action and sweat that has seeped into bedding – Maiko lies naked still and slumbering.

Jason takes a step right onto something, his foot directly on a substance half-sticky. A bad step. A gluey patch there.

He looks up to the ceiling wondering if something had leaked. Surely a bird could not have done its business there, flew in and made a mess. Surely not. A bat?

He bends to it and touches the sticky patch lightly with his finger and takes it under his nose and sniffs.

"Eww. Dude."

He knows.

No ceiling leak.

No bird or bat.

No small creature at all.

He wipes it off his boxers, disgusted … but he knows.

He is no longer sleepy; this has whipped him right awake. He's alert now and already adrenalin is pumping through him as if ready for fracas, ready for fight.

He goes into the main living room and Pete is already there, washed, dressed, a contrast to Jason's bed-hair disarray.

Jason's venom vanishes – this often happens when he sees Pete; look at his receding hairline; feels sorry mostly; yes feels sorry for him; he decides on no argument; his fists unclench; he looks at the older man and wonders: how did he get to be like that?

"You got up early," he says.

"Work to be done."

Jason glances around the room and sees that everything has been taken out of their cases and is standing in various parts of the room: guitars leaning back on stands, assured of themselves, inviting pluck or play, a drum kit, skins tuned and taut, sticks resting on snare, amps out and speakers aloft, things spread around strategically, recording equipment, all ready for tinkering, for experimenting, for use, for the coming together of their players again and for their purpose. Band.

"Where's the couch?"

"I took it outside."

"Why?"

"More room."

"How?"

"Stronger than you think."

The amount of strength needed to drag that all alone. The will. The perseverance. And at that hour of the morning.

Or did the mad bastard ever sleep? Who knows what kind of insanity he gets up to in the middle of his nasty nights?

Actually … Jason does … Jason does know.

"Did you eat something?"

"Just get her up and let's get started."

Leader.

Pete doesn't want to look at his bandmate. Could it be the shame? Or fear – Jason's strength, those ropey muscles if put to use.

Or is it that the bass he currently tunes needs all his attention now? The wide, silver key slowly turning and the string there tightening, reverberating when plucked, sending a low thrum that sets the very floor of the room a-tremble, as if an earthquake has come to collect them, or worse, some demon of the earth's depths is awakening to the day.

Jason saunters out the main door of the house and takes in the morning air. It is hot already. Not yet stifling, but give it a while. He takes deep breaths and surveys the scene. The previous night he had been out of his gourd, he remembers now – Maiko putting the tab on his tongue, and from then on a whirlwind, all kinds of wondrous worlds colliding, the real physical one of sexual union, and the mad map his mind had rogued.

He sees the grill of the night before and he walks to it.

Not a scrap.

He could've sworn there were bits of food left on it the night before. Pumpkin parts. Slices of beef. Had some animal come in the night and taken them? Some hungry thing? Probably. Easy pickings. But the welcome mat is more difficult to figure out. He could've sworn it was turned the other way round. The way it is turned now is not welcoming at all. It is saying quite the opposite, that you are not wanted here, not one bit. The inverse of welcome. What's that? *Begone!* Had Pete done this? Jason pictures him outside of his bedroom door, listening in, knowing what he had been up to. He has known Pete long enough, knows the behaviour patterns: spite, jealousy. Maiko doesn't know the half of it. Sick. That might be it, plainer. Is Pete *sick*? Are Maiko and Jason too? Are they full of some sort of sickness, some disease, or just some failing… to allow it, to allow it all to happen? Are they all in denial? Unpack that.

But it's too early. He needs to be inside and waking his lover and eating and showering and getting ready to make good music. It is the reason they are here. To create, not to murder each other. He turns the mat around. *Welcome.* He wanders back in.

"Did you clean up outside?"

"I only took the couch out."

"But the food and stuff."

"I didn't touch it."

"I left some vegetables. Meat. Right there on the grill."

"Maybe we ate everything ourselves. You were so fucking high. And anyway, some birds could've come and picked. This is the wild, mate. The wild."

"And the mat."

"The mat?"

"The welcome mat."

"What about it?"

"It had been turned the other way."

"You sure?"

"I'm sure."

Pete shakes his head, uncaring.

Bass, tuning keys: still he is turning.

Floor: still shaking, the vibrations.

"These speakers are too loud."

Is he trying to wake the sleeping princess with his thunderous vibrations? Is that the idea?

"Get her up."

It is. It *is* the idea. Get the whole house shaking. Spring the whole place into life. Music. There's work to be done.

"*Her?*"

"Yeah. *Her.*"

Maiko is awake and sitting on the futon naked. Already it is hot and she could quite happily go the whole day without any clothes at all. Jason wouldn't mind. But Pete? The poor man, he wouldn't have the stomach for it.

She should feel no sympathy for him but she has begun to worry.

She puffs on a cigarette, blows grey unsteady plumes around the room as Jason enters.

"He told you not to smoke."

"I remember."

"You are a very naughty girl."

"I am."

He sits beside her, takes the cigarette from her fingers and takes a long drag of it himself, a drag so deep he ends up coughing, his throat not quite prepared. When his spluttering ends he lets the cigarette hang from his mouth, 1940s noir pastiche, levity might regain him some composure.

He crouches over her.

She lies back, allowing it all, the Bogartziness, the brazenness.

Ash falls across her breast, neither of them brushes it away.

"The boss said that you are to get dressed. Get yourself ready."

"What if I were to stay like this all day?"

"I don't think the boss would be too happy."

Jason imitates Pete's British accent, "*There's work to be done, mate.*"

"Maybe he might like what he sees."

"Maybe he would be absolutely fucking astounded. Never seen such beauty before."

"Maybe he might be inspired to write a classic song."

"Maybe I gotta get going."

He laughs as he climbs off of her, places the cigarette back between her lips and goes to the door.

He tells her he needs a shower. They both do. The smell of their exertions permeates.

"I'll follow."

She is left there, finishing the cigarette. With no ashtray to be found she stubs it out on an old ornamental plate, she hopes it isn't worth much.

She goes to the window and stands there.

No houses around so no one can see her, in all her glory. She has been losing weight, and could do with a few pounds, but the cigarettes and the drugs and the alcohol don't give her much mind for food. She eats scraps, bits and pieces, like what an animal gets thrown, or like a feral feline that slinks to ransack backyard sacks.

She is in no rush. She knows Pete will be freaking out downstairs. But fuck him. She will be ready when she is ready.

She opens the window and a wisp of wind creeps in and caresses. She thinks of *chicken flesh*, the way it is said in her own language – she doesn't know how her bandmates might say it: those eruptions of pimples on the skin and the fine hair rising. It doesn't matter what it's called anyway, it just feels so good; she rubs her arms up and down, enjoying a mindful moment.

Something moving then.

She thinks she sees something moving in the bushes as she had done the previous day. She stares hard but she can see nothing.

Eyes? Eyes from before? Where have those eyes come from? Does she know those eyes? In the bushes. Hidden. But eyes, sure, yes. Were those flashes of eyes?

Maiko gasps and covers her breasts with her arms. She swiftly draws the curtains across, darkening the room – as much as it can be darkened this bright day.

She stands for a moment breathing heavily, controlling her sense of unease and wondering if she had actually spotted something.

Had she?

Or just her imagination?

All three of them: they are creative: Maiko, Jason, Pete. They are used to making things up. Letting their imaginations stampede. It is the reason they are there. To create. Something out of nothing. Experiment. Let loose. The basis for them being in this house: a house that for some reason feels inhospitable, as if it doesn't want them there and moans when they move about in it – can a house really give off such a frigid feeling? Or do they impose?

Is it the woods outside?

Imagination. It could be just that.

Imagination, its riot-runs.

Nothing there at all.

Figments.

But she is still hiding her breasts behind her arms, crouching down now, like an animal trying to hide from prey.

Pete has headphones on and is fiddling around with a synthesizer. Jason walks in, shirt open, and Pete gazes up at his ripped physique. *Buff.* Do people still say that? Pete thinks this as he ogles.

Jason can feel his eyes on him but cannot fathom its intent – what is that? Hunger? Disgust? Desire?

He sits on a chair and picks up a Stratocaster and plays.

"Where is she?"

"Showering … why?"

"Why what?"

"*Why* … do you want to go and take a look, or something? Have a peep?"

Pete looks at him. Disgust, yes, his gaze is one of disgust.

"No, actually. I don't. Bit too young for me. Bit too young for you too, mate."

"Or … maybe you'd prefer to just lie outside the bathroom door for a while? Listen in. The water flowing over her body. Picture it. Spill your evil seed to that."

Pete reddens. Looks are daggers.

"Those strings need changing."

Headphones are put on again, roughly.

"I know … strings need changing … I'll do it. I'll change the fucking strings. One by fucking one, dude. One by fucking one.

E.

A.

D.

G.

B.

E."

Jason knows Pete is no longer listening, the headphones cancelling everything out. Maybe for the best.

"You fucking freak."

Pete does not react.

He says it again.

"You fucking freak."

Pete hears nothing.

Maybe the headphones cancel his own terrible thoughts.

Jason changes the six strings, like he has been told to do.

Fights.

She remembers them from her childhood. So many fights. So many arguments, squabbles, tetchiness: commonplace.

School.

Home.

Bullies.

Victims.

Each and every.

All-the-time.

And actual blows. *Coming to blows*, yes. Slaps across faces. Welts. Kicks and *lashing out* – she had siblings, and this was how they grew, passed the days.

One memory often comes back to her, a usual moan (at night alone). She is in a little park, daytime, with her best friend, Naomi. They might be seven, eight at most, pigtailed, still plump, only caring about themselves and their play, no boys yet, a million miles away, only treats and tiaras.

Naomi did something to upset her: Maiko cannot remember the details. Too long on the swing? A refusal to push hard enough, for *higher, higher, higher*? Climbing up the wrong way of the slide?

And the two started to fight, actually wrestling each other to the ground, pulling on those braids, knees scraping on the hard brown dirt.

Naomi was stronger – used to such battles, her older siblings were male and almost malefic in their rounds of daily tormenting.

Naomi had her in a stranglehold.

"You will never make me cry."

"You will never make me cry, either."

But Maiko did cry, she capitulated.

It wasn't from the hurt; it wasn't from the pain, not from the scraped knees that were now smeared from the miniature streams of blood and had bits of grit stuck there already under the open skin.

No.

It was because Naomi's mother had come to collect her and had stood, appalled, her hand over her mouth, in complete shock: these young girls, these *good* girls whom she gave milk and cookies to every day, let watch cartoons, these, her little darlings, now rolling in the dirt and ... *betraying* their goodness.

That's when Maiko cried, when she saw the reaction of Naomi's mother.

The shame of it.

The utter shame.

They were supposed to be friends.

This was not the way the world was supposed to operate. You were supposed to fight your enemies. There were plenty of them to go round. Never any shortage of them. There were people that said bad things about your family. People that mocked you for whatever happened to be wrong with you, whatever ailed, your lazy eye, your crooked leg, your wet lap (classroom mishap). *That* way the world made sense, only *that way*: the acknowledgment and the fighting of enemies ... the hatching of plans for retribution. You didn't wrestle your best friends. You just didn't! What hope, what hope for humanity if life was to be lived like that?

Maiko moaned and wept, and Naomi released her, and Naomi's mother dragged her daughter away, scolding as firmly as she could, but struggling to find the appropriate words to do so. You didn't wrestle your best friends, what kind of animal ... ?

Maiko sat wounded. No other child in the vicinity. She made her way back home, darkness falling gradually like a stage curtain on the autumn evening.

She sobbed all the way home.

But it wasn't from the pain. It wasn't the open stinging knee-wounds and the bits of grit inside. It was from the shame. It was only the shame.

15

The house says: I have seen much pain, encased within these walls, and it takes pain to know pain.

16

The men, they spend a while making random music, none of it melodic or in any way coherent, none of it harmonious.

They are separate: instruments, paths, motives.

They cannot even hear each other.

Pete's synth sounds are heavy, bombastic. He hits the keys with unnecessary force, but the sounds are only in his own ears, for himself to hear. What is he telling himself?

Jason's sounds are breezy, guitar licks done with light fingering, as if they could float away and have no reason to stick around, will go and find a cooler place.

Pete is all scrunched up. His posture. His face. He would not be happy if he saw this – if he caught a glimpse of himself in some reflective surface he would compare himself to the others, the fine and the handsome. But this is the way he holds himself this morning. Hunched. Not fine, and certainly not handsome.

Jason looks relaxed. Like he doesn't give a shit about anything. The world could be collapsing around him; he is beyond caring. He knows they will never make what they want to make anyway, incapable, too much animosity, imbalance, even though they are here, even though they did make it this far. He remembers his own words in the van: *Genki will land us a good deal. We'll cut the record when we get back to the city. Tour later in the year. Things are going to start looking up. A breeze. Chill.* He doesn't believe in any of this. Why did he even say those things? Why even come here? The middle of nowhere. That's a phrase he'll have to teach his girlfriend.

The middle of nowhere. Why be here? To begin something? Or was it for it all to end? Why does he always trot out such lines? *Things are going to start looking up.* Trying to be optimistic. For whose sake?

Maiko enters, her hair wet, long legs bare, loose T-shirt, no bra. Jason winks at her.

"I'd love to wink back, but I've never mastered it. Sorry. I look either foolish or creepy doing it."

"Everyone looks either foolish or creepy doing it. That's maybe the point."

She thought they would both be more hungover. But they feel fresh enough, the shower having worked wonders. Maybe that's what the new songs could be about: simple things. Water. Water sluicing off the body. The ridding of dirt.

Pete pulls off his headphones and is immediately aware of the no-bra situation when she bends down to pick up a notebook marked *Lyrics.* For years she could not even say that word, *lyrics*, afraid to tackle the *l* and *r* combination: a tricky one that. But she's more confident now, her tongue tip hits all the right places, the sounds perfect.

Pete tries to keep his eyes on her eyes, not letting them roam along down her – she should know better though, she really should, cover herself up for Christ's sake. They needed to be able to concentrate: glimpses of forbidden flesh are the last thing he needs.

"Did you eat breakfast?"

She tells Pete that she had a nibble or two.

Nibble. She learned that. To her it sounded like *nipple.* Another funny-sounding word in English, but she liked it nonetheless. And *a bite to eat.* Or to *grab a bite. Grab.* That one seemed such an odd choice. *Grab.* But it's what Jason would say ... and what he would do.

"Good. We can get some actual work done today. Actual work."

Was what they did: *work*?

Would they get paid for this?

Where was Genki?

They hadn't heard from him for days.

Jason turns to Maiko, not even noticing the shape of her underneath the banana of the baggy Velvet Underground T-shirt (his).

"Did you know that a creature came in the middle of the night and took the scraps of food from the grill?"

Maiko, country girl, is not in the least surprised, shrugs it all off.

Jason likes her toughness, "You're not scared?"

"Not of wild animals, no. All you've got to be is sensible. You see a bear with her cubs you get the fuck outta there as quick as possible. You hope you're not smelled or seen. You hope you're not followed."

"Bears? No one said there were bears around here."

"You should be used to that, Montana boy."

"No one ever gets used to the idea of bears."

"Anyway, I'm sure they're nothing to worry about. Much bigger in the States." *Like everything*, she almost says, but lets it slide.

Pete already has had enough. Already they're talking tripe and he can't stomach it.

"Right. Fuck's sake. Enough with the jabbering. I've done the electric. I'll do the acoustic after."

Jason is pleased to have him annoyed like this – likes winding him up. The games they play. One up. One down. Winner. Loser. The word *band* suggests *solidarity*. But what's this? What kind of game is going on here? In this house that's not even theirs. What's this all about, really? The house doesn't even want them … can they feel that? Those draughts that lightly whip around their ears at odd moments … winds? Or are they whispers?

Outside.

Rustling sounds of something heaving through leaves and branches in the woods, treading, twigs cracking under footfall.

Animal?

No.

It is a man.

That suit has seen better days. It must have been worth something once. Once upon ... but now, it is tattered and frayed. Days. Nights in the woods. Trying to stay safe. Stay fed. Keep the spirits up and find a way out of this. He has been waiting for them. For the people to arrive. He has been spying. It is not his house. The house belongs to no one now, belongs to itself. He has taken the food from their grill and he finds a clearing and he sits there pulling the scraps out of his pockets and laying into them like he's never seen a bite before. He's famished. He's been so hungry. Days like this. It's been days now. Nights. Alone there. Fearful. Has he lost his mind? He's lost everything else. Nothing but the clothes on his back now, and they stink.

He eats the slices of onion, of pumpkin, of beef, they all taste wonderful, though he hardly gives them time on his tongue – he wants them down inside his stomach and fast, to stop the hurting, the cavernous noises his own body makes, the dizziness.

He'll make his way to the little stream when he's finished. He discovered this only yesterday. And the water there is so cool. So refreshingly cool. He dunks his head right into it, drinking thirstily, washing his face while he's at it. Washing his whole filthy head: the black hair itchy and so oily after only a few days. He's grunting like a caveman. What has he become? So far from home. So far gone. A man diminished, taken down.

The three musicians are sprawled out, different parts of the room, exhausted from their morning's exertion. The time flew. There is no clock in this room and perhaps that has helped. But Pete is surprised when he glances at his watch, and he feels almost proud. For all the notes they have played they have not produced anything noteworthy. But there are signs. These things will need time, gestation, and then they will be born. Pete is unusually upbeat about this. He must just keep the dark cumuli from gathering within himself. Keep himself in check, in other words. Head for sun and to the light and ...

But already an argument is in the pit of himself and swelling…

For things to grow you need the sun *and* the rain, the sun *and* the rain … isn't that how it works? How things grow? The sun *and* the rain.

"I think I need another shower," says Jason. "I thought it was supposed to be cooler in the mountains."

"We're not really *in* the mountains, Jason."

"Really, sweetheart. Where are we then?"

"At a slightly higher … what's the word?"

Pete the ex-language teacher, "Altitude."

"Attitude?"

"No, *altitude*. Attitude is something else."

This last remark is said with a sneer.

Jason is fanning himself with the lyrics notebook.

"Why didn't you fix it so that the place would have air-conditioning?"

"It's an old house, Jay."

"Or a few fans or something."

"Jesus Christ. Can't think of everything. Anyway, you'll never have … fans."

This is Pete's attempt at a joke. *Fans*. Maiko gets it, but it's not funny. Jason looks at her, tries to stop himself from rolling his eyes, and if he is to laugh it's at the childishness of the quip.

Pete sniggers to himself.

"I'm too hot for jokes, Pete. And I need a fucking drink."

They all three avoid eye contact and find things to fan against their faces. Sheets of paper, a dusty magazine that had been under the discarded couch, a different prime minister on the cover: things are always changing, but are they getting any better?

"You'd seen this place before though, right? You've been here before?"

Pete says nothing, closes his eyes.

It's hot. Hot, and he doesn't want to get bothered on top of that.

Finally, he chooses to say something, falling back into his usual stark monotone, "Jay, why don't you have that extra shower if you want. And have a look around, see if there are any electric fans lying about. There have to be some."

Jason looks at him suspiciously.

"And what are you two going to do?"

"We're going for a walk."

"A walk! In this heat? A fucking walk?"

Pete still has his eyes closed. He's thinking of horrors. He's thinking of what might be out there in the woods, what he might be able to see, what he might be able to fight. His thoughts often run that way; all he has to do is shut his eyes.

"Yeah. A walk. You want to come and meet a few bears?"

"Seriously. Why are you going out?"

Maiko senses tension again and she has to be the one to tame it. She silently moans about always being the one with the chair in one hand, the whip in the other.

"We think we might be able to find some mushrooms."

Jason knows.

Jason realizes.

He knows Pete's penchant.

He's seen that before.

He might not drink much, might take only the odd bump, but when those natural things spring out of the ground, he'll pluck them all right. The botanist. Shroom-head.

Pete still, eyes closed. Is he picturing himself in the woods already, walking with Maiko, living things sprouting?

"We won't be long. We can eat lunch when we get back. And maybe have a little cup of tea and all."

Pete smiles as he says this, as he pictures this. *A cup of tea and all.* He smiles at that.

Maiko blows Jason a kiss as she exits the room with the band leader.

Jason's lying flat on the floor, exhausted. He thinks the morning hasn't gone at all well. What kind of shit was that they were playing? And Maiko moaning. Why has she not got any proper words to sing? Just moaning, like a witch giving birth to her own familiar – fuck, even Yoko Ono wouldn't be at that avant-gar … *bage*. The whole thing is a disaster. But at least he's on his own for a while. He can take a quick nap. Take another shower. Find a fucking fan. He needs to find a fucking fan. *You'll never have fans.* Pete. Such a dick. Pete is such a dick. And he's not even funny. Good riddance. A bit of peace and quiet. Jason is soon snoring again. It doesn't take long.

Maiko says she got the phrase *a right moan* from Pete, got it from him, like an infection. He said his people, the British, were good at that, moaning about the weather, moaning about the government, whatever was on the front of the tabloids, anything at all, there was no end to it, *moaning*, there never is any end to it, it was what the people did best.

Or what was *on the box.*

That was another.

The *box* meant TV. Sometimes called *telly.* She's got such a mix: Jason's Americanisms, Pete's UK slang. What an education.

People would pay *good money* for that. *Good* money. A *right* moan. Things got qualified.

When Maiko mentioned all this to Pete one dull winter afternoon in a dull rehearsal room, he quoted Shakespeare, said he had learned the lines in school, and the character Caliban, which he said he related to:

You taught me language, and my profit on't
Is I know how to curse.

She didn't know how to respond to that. Modern English was difficult enough. Sometimes she knew he liked to keep her at bay. Keep *things* at bay. Words could do that. Language.

Quoting, he would say, was some kind of relief, that if you hadn't your own words, someone else's, someone wiser, yes, wiser words would fill the space, they were a comfort. He quoted often. How had he memorized so much?

And Maiko moans about this…
And Maiko moans about that…

Actually, Maiko doesn't moan about the government, or the weather, or what she sees on the TV (she hardly ever watches it; and she's never read Shakespeare, not even an easy-for-idiots translation).

Maiko's moans are more basic, more elemental; often they have no specific purpose, at all. They just come, out of her, emitted, like breathing, louder than sighing, from the centre of her, the innermost, sometimes from thinking, or over-thinking, and sometimes from not thinking at all, and with these two people, the two she is *lumped with*, the men (men?) what else is she going to do? A right moan. A right moaner. Maiko moans.

17

The house says: I'd prefer silence to be honest; the music, when it is not good, it hurts. It lacks soul. How can you spend so much time doing something and producing so little soul?

How can you do such a thing to walls? To where you are sheltered.

Such wails to walls is a crime. This place has seen enough of crime.

The house says: I would devour you… but you look like you will make a pretty good job of devouring yourselves.

The house repeats itself to itself.

On a loop.

18

"**G**ot water?"

Maiko pats her backpack to let Pete know they've got everything they need. She slings it around and slots her arms through the straps, ready for their hot hike.

Pete tells her not to worry if they run out, tells her there's a little stream he knows, if they need to refill.

"It's got cool water."

"So, you *have* been here before."

He clams up, as if he's been caught with his hand in the sweet jar, or some illicit magazine has been found under his teenage bed.

He puts on his hat for something to do – casts shade on a pale face blushing.

They set off through the woods, already the canopied cool feels one degree lower.

They take off their sunglasses, but the hats stay on, and Maiko sprays mosquito repellent on her arms and legs as they stroll. She gives Pete a few blasts of it too.

"Can't be too careful."

"You have a lot of interesting English expressions. Where did you pick them all up?"

"I learned from you. And Jason, of course."

"Of course."

"I listen carefully. I used to be a good student. Well, a clever student. But a lazy one. I always liked English. And music. That was all."

"I'm not a good teacher. Dangerous … some teachers … "

Maiko's not sure what he means by this and he goes no further to explain. He does that sometimes, just blurts things out. Things that are not really connected to anything else. Scraps of statements like dragonflies idling by.

Onward.

Cracking twigs under their feet.

The sounds of insects.

Phantom sounds of things too, creatures that might be moving through the undergrowth, but probably imagined, most probably not there at all.

"I also … "

How can she frame this?

She has to be careful around him. Prickly Pete.

"I also … pick up on things."

"Pick up?"

"Notice things. Tensions. Vibes."

He sniffs. Sensing trouble. Sensing confrontation. It is coming to him lightly, but it is coming to him nonetheless. She is a female of the species. They have their ways, they have wiles.

"And what, pray tell, have you gleaned?"

"Gleaned?"

"Learned."

"That something happened between you and Jason. But he won't tell me what it was."

"You asked him?"

She did. Just the night before.

They had been lying on their backs on the two single futons they had pushed together to make one. No blankets covered them in their hot new room, and even the flimsy sheets were cast aside, crumpled at their feet.

The couple lay there, bare, enjoying the drop of the evening's temperature on their sweat-soaked skin, just before Jason's slide into snores. Maiko had propped herself up on her elbow and looked at her lover in the dark. She rubbed his shoulders gently – she had something to ask him, but how was she to get it out?

Jason had his eyes closed, enjoying her touch, almost maternal it was, lovingly light, it wouldn't be long before it lulled him off to sleep. She asked him to tell her about the two of them, the men, the friends, before she had come along. Pete and Jason. The music. What they had made. As a couple, a pair, what they had made together.

He found a ridge on the inside of his left cheek to chew as he considered her question, but he was annoyed that he was not allowed to drift off, his work for the day was done.

"Why? Why do you ask?"

"Because I just want to know."

He let a little time tick by, and was cautious in his reply.

"We were fine. But you made things better. Genki was right to push for you. We needed sex appeal. The female kind."

She slapped him playfully on the shoulder. "Is that all I am to you? Sex appeal?"

His eyes were open fully then, staring at the ceiling.

"Think of it like when Nico joined the Velvets."

She wasn't about to let the reference derail her, she waited for him to carry on regardless.

"Warhol knew that Nico would make the band more special, not just because of her good looks, the blonde contrasting against the coolly black-clad, but her deep voice too, her attitude, her mystique."

Jason seemed almost taken aback by his own eloquence – perhaps it was rock history that could only make him this way, everything else, life, its messiness, invariably got garbled in his mouth, things usually came out in confused clumps. They were too young to be so in awe of rock dinosaurs, Jason and Pete, too young to like the things they did – Maiko never understood it. Their peers would never go for lame guitars and real drum kits. When The Strokes and The White Stripes swaggered into the new millennium kicking out their jams with a rock reprisal, Jason was still a child. It all seemed unlikely. Or maybe Pete and Jason just liked being the minority, being different – the past was perhaps a consoling place for them in that it was somehow comprehensible, unchangeable, the present was ever-messy, the future always unknown.

Jason was stuck in the groove of his spiel now: The Velvet Underground. Maiko doubted his fly-fishing father could've been the source of any of that.

"Lou Reed might not have liked it all that much to begin with … Nico, an imposter."

"And Pete?"

"Pete's just fucking grumpy. And weird. And a bit lost. He's told me weird snippets from his youth. His father was some kind of wandering Welsh preacher, religious maniac. And he had an uncle, weird scientist kinda dude, who told him all about drugs, plants and stuff. Imagine telling that to a kid. That it was OK to smoke weed. The uncle raised him, some kind of hippy. 1960s, Timothy Leary vibe."

"What about his mother?"

Jason shrugged. Was never told.

He went on, "So Pete was trying fucked-up shit from an early age. It messed with his brain. He has mood swings."

"No shit."

Maiko witnessed that for herself, on many occasions, the effects – Pete swings, for sure.

"He hasn't been diagnosed with anything, as far as I know. His coming to Japan was to be a kind of re-birth. Get far from home. Put the botany and shit aside. No drugs. Start on music. Which is the only thing that seems to soothe him."

She kept her eyes on Jason's eyes – the room dark, but vision accustomed: she could see that he was serious now, and worried, too.

"You saw how angry he got with the magic box. If it was *his* magic box it would be another story, naturally. He'd have more control. But because it's mine … he resents it. Like I said, he's weird, controlling. And annoying. And bossy. And he gets irritated when things don't go his way."

"For example?"

"Recording. Song-craft."

Her next question was to be a daring one. But she couldn't stop herself.

"What about you two … intimately?"

There.

It was out now.

The question that she had really wanted answering.

How long had that been brewing inside?

She could see his throat bobbing as if something got suddenly stuck. What kind of regret was lodged in there, and choking?

"Look, sometimes people take too many drugs, experiment, do stupid things … mistakes. Forget about Pete. Let's just make his goddamn album. Who knows, we might make even some money."

He kept talking, as if to get further away from her question.

"I know a guy who wants me to do some soundtrack work, an independent filmmaker, if it fails with Pete. We've got to keep our options open. Let Pete sort out his own shit. And there's plenty shit that he needs to sort out."

Jason turned then to kiss her, as if that was to be an end to it.

"I'm all yours now. Got it?"

She smiled, smiled him some sort of affirmation. But it was not convincing. It swayed neither of them. They soon succumbed to the lateness, to their tiredness, and they soundly slept.

A walk through the woods.

A hot day.

It all continues.

Pete's curiosity:

"Did he talk about me?"

"He always talks about you."

"All good things?"

"Of course. You've been playing together for a long time. Since you both first came to Japan, right? Language teachers?"

It's Pete's turn to get cast back into a memory and it's not such a recent one. A typical late-night Japanese *snack bar:* a small drinking establishment for boisterous, boozy *salarymen* who had not gone home to their wives but had stayed out to continue their libations. A group of be-suited employees, foreign and native alike, all enjoying a drunken karaoke session, and beer and *sake* got poured and quickly downed.

Pete had been in a sensible shirt and tie, but flecks of sauce from the *yakitori* he had been eating spoiled the effect, made him look dirty. There was always some flaw with him. Always something just that little bit off.

He was looking at the digital device that let the chooser identify songs from a playlist, his fingers pushing on the buttons – so many, so many songs out there, endless, and being drunk he wanted only to possess them all, the way euphoric drunks are wont, even the songs that were well out of his vocal range, and the ones he hardly knew. The drink gave him courage, lent him esteem. The drink made him even half friendly.

"Need any help?"

He didn't know this man. He'd seen him. The same language school; they'd passed each other in corridors. But this was the first time they'd spoken.

Pete got flustered: fingers on the digital device all fidgety then, an attack of nerves. He said that he was going to do a Bowie number. And the man who introduced himself as Jason, asked him which one.

"Starman".

"Need a Mick Ronson by your side?"

"You know your 70s rock."

"I'm a guitarist."

"Welcome to the club."

At that moment Pete took his eyes off the digital device to look fully at the man with the American accent. The size of his eyes expanded in surprise, overcome by the sheer physical delight. His hands developed a tremor, and he tried to conceal it. If there had been music playing, and he had been singing or playing along, things would have been different, would have been calmer. But he had no such crutch to lean on. He felt exposed.

Jason pointed to the karaoke screen in the corner of the bar.

"Looks like we're up."

The two arose and went to the performance area as their drunken colleagues encouragingly cheered. A swaying Japanese man in a crumpled business suit reluctantly handed over the microphone. Before the music kicked in Jason leaned on Pete in the classic Bowie-leaning-on-Ronson pose.

"Like this, wasn't it?"

Pete giggled as the intro started, giddy with a burgeoning musical – or was it sexual? – excitement.

Narrow winding trails: Pete and Maiko walking.

A hum of something near, it could be a nest of hornets – the Japanese variety they knew were the most dangerous in the world.

So much they cannot see.

So much hidden, to survive, to be successful.

They come across a long wooden fence near what appears to be some kind of disused farm outhouse – cultivated fruit plants grow along the slats of the fence, and the pair stop before a green bush flush with green berries.

The place is open, able to receive sunlight, and Maiko has to shield her eyes from the sudden luminosity.

She is confused. As if she's just wandered into a Grimm Brothers' tale, a house made of confectionery could be just around the corner.

"What's this?"

"My secret garden."

"You ... grew these?"

Pete looks proudly at the bush and Maiko pushes him to explain. He cannot now deny that he has been here before. Definitely. Definitely. He knows this place. He knows it well.

"I came here many times before. I know this place, sure."

He bends to inspect the fruit, almost caresses them, as if he's crafted each individual berry himself.

"There was a boy I knew, used to live here. That's how I knew about the house."

A boy.

She is picturing the skinny male rock fan following Pete out of that filthy toilet, the smudge of white under Pete's nose. The woozy excitement they emitted as they passed her.

Pete looks embarrassed, as if she's guessed correctly. He takes off his sunglasses and wipes the sweat off his eyes, all the while trying not to make eye-contact with her. He puts the glasses in his pocket, his attention fixed on the bush.

"It's OK. You can talk to me."

He lets a moment pass, then plucks one baby berry from its cradle.

"It's their season. Or almost."

Maiko puts her own sunglasses on her head, moves closer to inspect.

"What are they?"

"Gooseberries."

"I've never seen them before."

"They're not native to here. But I was able to grow them."

"Right ... *botany*. Can I eat one?"

"If you want."

She plucks a bigger, riper one from the bush, pops it in her mouth, but she spits it straight back out.

"Jesus."

"They're an acquired taste. Take a bit of getting used to."

Pete eats one, shows not the slightest reaction to the tartness.

They sit for a few minutes in silence, resting, taking in their surroundings. Pete takes out a penknife and starts to cut thin slices off the stems. He puts them in a Ziploc bag which he tucks away again in his backpack.

Maiko watches his every move.

"What are they for?"

"We can add them to our dinner. Very nutritious. Will give you great … energy. Creativity."

He sits back again and pops another berry in his mouth.

"You don't think they're bitter?"

"I do. But everything in life is bitter."

He's deadly serious – she was going to laugh, but it's no joke, his expression is pinched, severe, she wouldn't now dare.

"There's an idiom. *Playing gooseberry.* Or, *he's a gooseberry.* Do you know what that means?"

She doesn't, but she knows damn well he'll mansplain it, and she can feel a sense of animosity arising in his tone.

"It's British, I suspect," he says. "To *play gooseberry* is to be in the way of a couple. A couple who'd rather you weren't there. They want to be private … but the gooseberry is there, blocking the path."

He looks at her to gauge her reaction, but she's giving nothing away.

Mood swings.

She knows to be wary of him. He's not like Jason. The American is simple, upfront. He said it himself about Pete: *Controlling. Weird.*

"It's an old term for a chaperone. Someone who had to take care of a young woman, say, and didn't want the suitor to be too … amorous. To give the couple some moment of privacy while out on a walk, the chaperone would pretend to pick a gooseberry from a bush, giving the pair the opportunity for a sneaky kiss. But it became a very negative term. Someone who gets in the way, especially in the way of love, in the way of passion."

Maiko is frowning, trying to follow.

"In the States it would most likely be called *a third wheel*. And another expression is *going gooseberry*. This means to steal clothes off a washing line. Like … a vagrant might do."

Further frowns.

"What's a *vagrant*?"

"Like *homeless*. Like what we'll be if we don't start to make money from our music. I don't want to be going back to teaching shitty English lessons again, Maiko."

Bitterness still, and Maiko gets the sense that he's not finished. That he could let loose a litany of sore points, sour grapes.

"Or Genki. If we don't make money *for him*. Ha! For his plush apartment."

Pete pauses, smiling, then spits out something that had been caught between his teeth, a piece of gooseberry flesh.

"Maybe he's homeless already," he laughs at this, taking delight in his own words.

"I doubt that. He always lands on his feet."

"Don't be too sure. Misfortune can happen to anyone."

The line sounded rehearsed, fake, but it got Maiko to thinking. Misfortune *can* happen to anyone. And she cares about people. She cared enough to say *yes* to be in a band in the first place. Just because she could sing. Is that all she can do? Why couldn't she have gotten a proper job? Like her family had wanted. They were work-obsessed. But what was wrong with that, if your work meant something? Why not be obsessed by it? She didn't even fully know what her father did. Something to do with energy research, or fuel, some part of a team that was trying to move away from nuclear … hydrogen! Something like that, wasn't it? Hydrogen? Her father was clever. Remarked at dinner once that it was the way of the future. Hydrogen, or was it carbon storage? What did those things even mean? What future? Is that why she is a disappointment to him? Because she never asked him about what he did; she had been too incurious. He never actually *said* it. He never actually said that she was a disappointment. But it was that look in his eyes. She was clever enough to go to university, but she had never bothered. That was what hurt him most. She couldn't be bothered. And, if all she felt that she could do well was sing … if that was all … like if all that she could do was …

They sit in silence on the forest floor. Pete thinks she's mulling over what he has said to her, gooseberries, idioms … but she's on a different plane entirely.

There's a sorrowful look about him, as he stares at the bushes, at *his* bushes.

"They take a long time to grow, to get right. All my efforts. My secrets are there, under the gooseberry bush. Ha!"

"What?"

"It's another idiom. *Under the gooseberry bush.* It has two meanings. One is the answer parents would give to children if they ever asked where babies came from. The other is old slang for pubic hair."

"See, you are a good teacher."

"No. Too dangerous. Who knows what I have buried under there, to make them grow so well."

He laughs to himself, and Maiko thinks the more he speaks the less she understands him. The more time she spends with him, the more obscure everything feels. Like he is the opposite of everyone else she has ever known. Sure, he can list quaint phrases, explain expressions, but he can't really reveal anything about himself – everything seems buried, or are codes meant to be deciphered?

Jason: basic appetites, fewer games, you knew what he wanted – if it wasn't already obvious by his behaviour, he would just come out and say it, or do it. *Grab a bite.* Grab her by the ass.

But this one. Their *leader.* An altogether different beast.

"Look … can I ask you something?"

Some full-throated thing squawks somewhere in the woods, another hidden thing.

"Last night…when Jason and I were…you know…were you…?"

Jason splashes cold water on his face and wipes himself dry with a towel. He leaves the bathroom and starts walking around the house, snooping, snooping, but languidly, from room to room, at ease.

He stops in front of a *butsudan* altar and gazes upon it.

How different it is to anything back home. If his father was beside him, he'd have a million questions – what does that ornament mean, and that Buddhist symbol there? What's that? And Jason would have no answers, still clueless to so much of the culture, even though he's been here…how long now? But it doesn't seem to faze him all that much. He is going to make some music with his partners. Keep life simple. If it works out, it works out, and if it doesn't, then fuck it. He can always go elsewhere. (Maiko never understood such a sentence, its construction, why *always*, why *always* used there in such a way, it made no sense to her – or was it some philosophical thing, that Westerners *always* had a way out, because they were Western, and these two were white male Westerners, there would *always* be options?) Jason was tied to nothing, tied to no one. And if it meant going back home to rivers and crisp Western mountain air, then fine, there was nothing wrong with that either. He'd been running long enough. From what? Nothing. For the sake of it. Some wanderlust, perhaps, if even that. Or just because he is still young. *Ish.* Not that young anymore. His father, were he around, would be pressing him to *get sensible*. That was one of his stock phrases. *Get sensible.* It meant settling down, with *a nice girl.* And what was that? Or *who* was that?

He wanders to the other side of a room and studies the *kakejiku* on the wall. This hanging scroll was more comprehensible, full as it was of typical Japanese images: a turtle, a crane, Mt. Fuji, the setting sun. Easier to interpret. And just as he is about to leave it and investigate some other corner of the house, he sees a long wooden box at the side of the room. Now, what could be in there? Perhaps he did spend too much time watching Scooby Doo as a kid, this nosiness he's developed, this proclivity for peeking into dark corners.

But there is nothing at all cartoonish about what he finds when he opens the box: a long, silver sword that looks in gleamingly good condition. On closer inspection he notices specks of dried blood on it, right near the top of the blade. What might that have pierced? That tip. What might that have penetrated?

Or whom?

Quizzical, her expression now. And patient too.

But…

A complete change comes over Pete. Not sorrow. No. It's something else. Something beyond all that, it could be another person. Perhaps it is.

The small man rises from where they've been sitting and looks bigger than he's ever been. What strange shadows are cast from his frame, but hardly any light breaks through the forest in the first place, so how can that be?

And he moves, this new creature, lurching slowly, moving away from her, trance-like, his gait more a deep-water wade.

She trots after him, catches up, walks beside him, her look beseeching, baffled, but beseeching.

Pete is zombie-like, unblinking, has he taken something? A shroom already? No. She never saw any of that. He has the stagger of something that has just crawled out of a Haitian grave, a voodoo curse upon his cursed bones.

Maiko is not beseeching now; she's fucking freaking out.

"Pete! Talk to me! I'm sorry! I didn't mean…"

She reaches out for his hand, wants to pull him back to her realm, but he turns on her.

Hard across her face he smacks her, hard. She falls to the forest floor. Behind her hair-mess – when she peeps back out to the world – she has a look of abject horror.

He stands over her, menacingly. A creature about to devour another.

"Never question me! Never question what I do!"

Maiko is in tears on the ground, her salty drops hitting the dry earth.

She is flabbergasted, floored, frightened.

Pete's hand starts to tremble again. He cannot get rid of that. Nerves. Or excitement? He never can tell. As a youngster his bowels would tremble from one or the other, could let loose at any moment, catch him off guard, often he stood in the middle of his own stink. He got lashes from his father for that, a switch of birch across the back. Son of a bitch. That's what Jason would say. Son a bitch. But Pete was a son of a ...

He's shaking his head now, surprised at what he's done. It didn't feel like his doing.

And yet ...

It was the same strong right hand. The one that plucks strings, fingers on black and white keys, the hand that pulls hard on himself to an almost rawness when he listens in on other people's moans.

He steps back. Back from his prey. He does not know what he has done. He knows, sure, but to what extent?

He turns and runs, back, through the dark forest.

How can it be so dark – it is morning and birds are singing and the day should be a blessing upon them: *A land of darkness, as darkness itself; and of the shadow of death, without any order, and where the light is as darkness.*

He pants as he runs.

He just has to get away from there.

He believeth not that he shall return out of darkness, and he is waited for of the sword.

Job 15:22.

He has shrunken back to his familiar size again. He was big there briefly, just for a second, briefly big, impressive. The hitting of another. Smack across her face when she least expected it. Smack. That got her. Bitch. Fucking bitch. But he is small again. And he is as frightened as the woman he made victim. *Because they turned back from him, and would not consider any of his ways.*

The forest floor. She gets to see it all now, close up. There are little things crawling. Tiny ants. Is that what they are, ants? All industry, a society making sense, until trod upon.

Her vision is blurred, from tears, from shock. And there is something long and wormy crawling there too. Some kind of centipede or caterpillar. Is it the season? She is not sure. She hardly knows the difference between all these things. Country girl, yes. But she was always looking at the bigger picture (she could *always* leave, go West), not focused on the minutiae.

She lays there. Not far from the gooseberry bush. The sour taste is still in her mouth. The taste of bad fruit. The taste of a bad experience. What should she do now? She should get up. She should rise and deal with it. But she stays longer. Smells the earth. The reality of the place. Nature. She grew up in a place like this and then her family moved to the city because her father got a better job. People are always on the move. Things, things are always on the move. Things never stop for a moment to take other things in. She was doing that now, a mindful moment, that was not planned, alone on the forest floor, after being knocked down by her bandmate. By her leader. Taking things in. How would she get over this?

She had seen a nature documentary – it was something Jason had been watching. In the clip, a mouse was out foraging in the woods, minding its own tiny business. Its whiskers were twitching and it became aware that something was awry. Its instincts had been correct, because a snake was slithering, stealthily approaching, readying to strike. So slowly it moved, that snake, and the camerawork was riveting, so much so that even Maiko got caught up in it, her eyes as wide as Jason's. So slowly it moved, and the watchers unblinking.

The snake pounced, but, amazingly, the tiny mouse leapt two meters up into the air at the precise and preserving moment, and the snake, shocked, reeling, was left whirling back on its back, had no inkling that such a thing was ever going to take place. How could it, how could it have possibly foreseen? You think you know your enemy. The mouse continued to bounce its way out of the place. Who would have thought such tiny legs could make a jump so high. Jason whooped with delight. It was a marvellous scene, and she too was undeniably impressed, but her only response was to raise her eyebrows in admiration. Jason had whooped. It was something his people did. *His* people. For victory. She could never be like that. Shows of emotion. Responses like that. None of her business. What did victory mean to her? Would it be in the making of a good song? A fine piece of music. Art? Would that be *victory*? Something to cheer about? To whoop? She envied him his ease, so underdeveloped a character, hardly making an impression, despite his bulk, and stirred by as little as the jumping of a panicked mouse. She envied him. She envied him his life-affirming whoop, his life-grabs, his guilelessness.

Forest floor.
She lies there still.
She should have jumped.
She should have been a brave little mouse.
But she is a singer in a band with two others … and now she is lost.
She should have been a brave little mouse.
She should have jumped, two metres high.
But still, she lies there.
Forest floor.

Maiko once heard moaning behind the shed of their old country house. House in the country. Not *country house*.

When she went to investigate, she found an old couple, neighbours, at it.

They must have been in their sixties, the pair of them. They had most of their farm-garments off and they were groping hungrily at one another, and laughing – yes, in the midst of their gruff passion there was much laughter. Maiko started laughing herself, and had to cover her mouth with her hand so as not to be heard. She should have fled from that shed, but she didn't. She stayed to watch, right up until its juddering conclusion. How funny it was, and how life-affirming that too, like Jason's whoop of joy; this break in the day for a couple who had been married for decades.

How young was she then? Eleven? Twelve?

The scene could have been traumatizing. But instead it soothed her.

Her father and mother were at work most of the time. It is all they ever knew. If they took a break it was probably for cigarettes or coffee from vending machines. Not to hungrily grope at one other.

Maiko liked the moans of the neighbours. She wondered if she would have the same kind of moans in her future, the same kind of hunger. Some wrinkly old man, or old woman, it didn't matter, didn't matter which, pawing at her; wrinkly things, yeah, just pawing, just pawing at each other, wants, gropes and grunts.

Hunger: it wasn't always such a bad thing.

19

The house says it accommodates only the right people. It would not let in those who would sully or soil.

A house can tell the difference.

Sometimes a house can feel sick, sick from the sick ones that roam about in it, like viruses.

The house wants to projectile-vomit them out.

Begone!

20

She lies there yet, and yet she sobs.
What happened?
What was all that?
He had just run away.
Pete had hit her.
And then he had fled.

Rustling then. Always something on the move. Sometimes it is small, a mouse, a mole, or smaller still, a stag beetle on its warpath, armoured, ready. Or bigger. Something bolder. A wild boar, a serow...

It can't be Pete. He has gone. So, what then? What now? What issues next?

Maiko's fear escalates; she's frozen stiff with fear.

On this hot day: frozen. Just another oddness.

What is it, that rustling? Some lost human on some lonesome trail? Nothing odd about that. People get lost all the time.

Rustling. And it approaches...

Pete runs through the trees, releasing guttural groans. He sobs too, face foul with weeping, sobbing heavier than the woman he scared (in his eyelids the shadow of death), eruptions of snot too from his nostrils. *Nose water!* That's what they called it here! Water from the nose. So literal at times, the Japanese. He's learned things. He has. *I should have been as though I had not been; I should have been carried from the womb to the grave.* He runs. Why did he do that? To scare her? To make her his? Why? *And everyone that was in distress, and every one that was in debt, and every one that was disconnected, gathered themselves unto him; and he became a captain over them.*

The gooseberry bush. Things buried.

His face is sweaty, his look anguished, like he's seen a ghost, or like he's seen himself. This is the way of the woods, day or night, and you will only recognize such when you encounter, head on – only ever truly recognize anything on such encounters, head on, no, no, no, much closer than that, nearer: the face to face.

Himself.

Maiko, petrified, a forest.

She looks around frantically – wondering whether to run or to remain.

She stays. Her spot. Near the gooseberry bush. Rooted. Near the fruit she could not stand to eat. Something brushes past foliage again. Nearing. And then …

A figure emerges.

Maiko screams aghast at the sight of the grimy presence, this decrepitude of man, coming at her now, approaching – she can smell him already, already the filth upon her, vagrant, pitiful homeless creature, putridity, she's seen this man before, outside the van, as they drove here, and then they'd driven quickly on, they'd left him for dust.

He speaks to her, softly.

Her own language.

A voice she knows!

A voice she knows!

"Maiko."

She was ready to scream again, she was ready to … but did he just say her name? And sweetly?

Astonished.

Again, "Maiko."

"Genki?"

"Yes, it's me."

From head to toe, she examines.

He is still a few metres away, but through her tears, yes, it's him, it's most definitely him! Genki! The name meaning: *a cheerful robustness*, not *decrepitude.*

He walks towards her slowly, cautiously, as a human would to a wild animal … or is it a wild animal to a human?

He does not want to upset her.

"What happened to you?"

"What happened to me? Where to begin? Pete. Pete happened to me. All this. It's Pete. All this."

She lunges at him then, throwing her arms around him in a great big bear hug – she can handle the smell now, it's only him, it's only her Genki, he's not putrid at all, how could she have thought …

And she shivers in fits of tears and with the joy of this embrace.

Through the undergrowth.

Past the leaves.

Brushing against branches.

Unsettling ferns.

Pete is running the final steps to the house.

When he gets to the front door he turns the welcome mat around, reversing Jason's work. It means *Unwelcome* now.

Why would Pete do that? Why does Pete do anything? He has come to make music. He is not making it well.

Pete is about to step in the door when a swooshing sword slices the air before him, and he has to pull back to avoid getting his head chopped off. Shocked out of his trance, Pete is brought back into the day.

"Jesus Christ!"

His uncle had never minded him swearing; something his father abhorred: the Lord's name, taken in vain. But his father was never around to hear it. His uncle stayed, stayed with his herbs and hedonism, raised him, on philosophy and foolishness, but Uncle stayed – he could swear about Jesus till his heart was warm with the explosion, with the expulsion of it.

"What the fuck are you doing, Jay?"

Jason is holding the sword.

"Sorry. I didn't mean to swing it so hard."

"You could have fucking killed me!"

Jason tries to alleviate; he's shuffling again, a soft shoe shuffle on the wooden floor of the vestibule – how do you apologise for nearly killing your bandmate, the person you've known longest, in a land where you don't belong?

Unwelcome.

"Just … you know … in case it was a bear."

Pete assumes the face of the band's leader, it's the grim back-of-the-van face; gone has the gooseberry-bush-terror face, when he spat down on the terrified female, smacked her hard, knocking the wind out of her sails, a peg or two, brought down a peg or two, but that's gone now, he is almost calm, breathless from running, but he is almost calm.

He looks at Jason without anger, pitying the American's stupidity, symptomatic of the times perhaps: a lost loon with a weapon in a place he shouldn't be: was there ever anything so American, this recklessness, not knowing your own strength, was there ever anyone so typically American?

"It's a sword, Japanese *katana*."

"I can see that, Jay."

Pete takes water from his backpack and gulps it down.

"You don't look all that surprised. You've seen this sword before, haven't you?"

Pete gives nothing away.

"How? When?"

"Go get me a beer."

Jason stands. He is beautiful. Tall and photogenic. But there is no one else to see that, only Pete, and it's best to bring him down too, bring Jason down a peg or two, bring everybody down, down, down everybody. Can't all be bloody beautiful and brandishing weapons. Come down to Pete's size, come down and be ugly with Pete. Be breathless and be unfit and be utterly ugly.

Deplorable.

Disposable.

Be ugly.

"Go get me a beer, I said. Now!"

Stern.

The leader.

Boss of the band.

But *band* means *solidarity*, means …

Jason succumbs to the shorter man, sword or no he goes off in the direction of the kitchen, subservient.

Pete straightens himself. Heads to the main music room, stands and surveys: all the stuff in there, so underused, annoyance now, he is full of annoyance now, brimming, baleful, bileful, there has been no progress made. None. How long had they been there, in this house?

They had come to make music.

Not to break up.

To break down.

Jason returns and hands the man his beer.

"Where's Maiko?"

"She's coming."

"Did something happen?"

"Like what?"

Jason smiles, wanting to regain something. He thinks he knows, he's guessing anyway, yeah, sword or no sword, he can make a stab at it, "Oh, I see. You hit on her and she rejected you."

Pete is alarmed for a second until he realizes that Jason said *hit on*. Not just *hit*. It meant something else entirely.

Hit on. Fuck Jason and his Americanisms. They were ruining the very language.

Hit on. My arse. Cunts.

Everything about them made the language violent. *Hit on.* They couldn't do a gig without it *bombing*, or *killing*, or *nailing* it, or *destroying*.

Pete takes a slow drink from the cool can. He's trying not to get drawn into mind games, trying not to (he'd rather be making music), but he fights back nonetheless:

"Fuck you."

"Ha! It's true, isn't it? You came on to her. You tried to touch her. Or you showed her your little winkle and she laughed at you."

Pete cannot wash away his look of spite with gulps from the can of beer. His face is sweatier than ever: the drink has only brought out more beads on his brow.

Jason plays with the sword, assumes the position of a samurai warrior.

The two of them: what games they play, assuming roles, assuming positions.

"It's great, this thing. I found it in a box. Look powerful, don't I?"

He could be eight years old, a child in the playground, other American idiot kids envious of him.

"Look, mate, put that thing down. If you're not going to use it then don't hold it. You'll only look weak. Weaker."

"There's dried blood on it."

"Really. How shocking."

Pete walks right past him, beer in hand, out the living room door.

He heads for the bathroom: the best thing he can do now is shower the morning away. Purge. Start the shitty day again. They have music to make, and he needs a clear head to do so, not sit around listening to Jason's bullshit – he looks like a child with the sword, as big as he is. *Look powerful, don't I?* If you hold something like that (like holding a guitar) you have to be prepared to use it, and you have to use it properly. It's no use just posing. No use assuming the stance. You have to commit. Guitar: you play. Sword: you slay. Otherwise, stay away. Fucking betraying cunt.

Jason drops the weapon carelessly on the floor. He takes a pre-rolled joint out of the magic box, lights it, sits back and smokes.

It's his hand that is shaking now, not quite able to process what just happened, or how he had let it all come about. What is he even doing here? Jason Kiberd. What brought him to this country? A year abroad. That was the initial plan. Turned into more. Many more. The women were easy. Easily attracted because he was everything the Japanese males were not: tall, fair, blue-eyed, unafraid to let passionate thoughts be released, uninhibited, unembarrassed. He should be wading in a river with his father. That's where he *should have been*. His mind always veers, like a bowling ball in the side channel, not going in the direction you wanted it (his father had shown him how, Dirk's Bowling Alley, even gave him a first sip of beer there when no one was looking) – the words *cancer* and *pancreas* never far from him … and what if it's all hereditary?

Pancreas. Fuck. What a way. What a way to finish up. If he had stayed with his father maybe the river would have washed away the cancer. Washed away all the pains. Given it to the fish. The slippery fish. They used to try and catch with rods and nets and bait … they used to …

But he must not dwell. It hurts. Even the words. Even "Montana". He doesn't want to hear it. Not now. He's too far away. He'll have to get back.

And what just happened?

Pete's eyes.

Go get me a beer, I said. Now!

And he did. Shit.

And Maiko. Where is she? And does he even care about her? He does, sure, but like … how much? When he said the word *marriage*, he meant it, didn't he? Or was it another thing to just say, to get his wicked way? How much? Jason: is he serious? Serious about anything?

He picks up a guitar and starts to strum but grows immediately glum. Dissatisfied with the first few tepid chords, he flings it aside. It lands next to the sword on the living room floor and lies there.

Both are useless now. Guitar and sword. If not used properly, useless.

And he feels that way, too. A useless person.

So he smokes.

And he coughs a little.

Can that affect the pancreas too, or just the lungs?

How little he knows, how fucking little.

A high school education, well … he attended classes, and college, well … he attended there too, enough to scrape together something meritorious, enough to get an entry into another country and a job that paid reasonably well.

He smokes again.

And the haze that fills the room and fills his head is a weak balm, but it is a balm nonetheless, so he'll take it.

There is a sense of relief in that Maiko can speak in Japanese and really express herself. Speaking in English all the time to Jason and Pete can be exhausting, the concentration it requires: phrases, idioms, vagaries. The new kind of singing she wants to try will have no language at all, just moans, just great moans of feeling, which make more sense to her now; she is sure this is the way to proceed, moaning her mind out. Words need too much thought, have connotations, meanings that can be picked apart like old crows at rubbish sacks, disruptions, disruptions of words, but if you just moan along with the music, make sense to yourself first … but what will an audience make of it? Will they moan along? Still, still, this is how she'll proceed, she is sure. All these words and all this talk and everyone at it, opinions, opinions, and showing off, there were too many of them, too many words, it didn't matter the language they were uttered in. She had heard of an Icelandic band that does such a thing, songs with words moaned in a kind of non-language – Pete surely must've mentioned this, she cannot remember their name, she needs to find out, check them out, remind herself. The mouth, making sounds, but not words – actual words are too sneaky, hard to keep hold of, slippery, those of another language even more so, like eels, dark things that don't want to be caught, preferring the murky depths. Eels. Crows. The animal kingdom. Kingdom of words. Babel. It is a comfort that Genki is speaking to her in words she doesn't have to think too carefully about, that flow or fly up to her and stay with her and that she doesn't need to decode or make deductions, sentences that just solidly sit and make no play to slip away.

"I know. I stink."

"I don't understand any of this. What happened?"

"I came here weeks ago, with Pete. He said he wanted a quiet place to record, to get away from the city. He said he had a lot on his mind. Being honest with him, I told him that I wasn't sure the band was going to be a success, unless he pushed you more to the fore, have you on every flyer, every notice. You had to be the centre of everything. He didn't like that one bit. But he said the house, some valuable time spent in the country, would bring the three of you together. And he knew a place that was owned by some boyfriend he had in the past. The place was left vacant for years. Pete convinced us that he had a key and had permission to use it."

Maiko hangs on his every word, her nods telling him yes, to go on, go on, proceed.

"He convinced me to come here. So we drove. We didn't tell either of you. We wanted it to be a surprise. When we got here, I thought the house was too small, but Pete insisted that we use it, that the quiet of the countryside would be good for us. He said he knew the area well, and that you'd bond, as a band, and make new exciting music."

Genki stops to let Maiko take it all in. She hands him her water bottle and urges him to drink from it. Soon she will feed him herself, take him to the kitchen, nourish – even if she has to miraculously produce milk from her very own breast, she will somehow find a way to nourish him.

He drinks greedily and continues.

"That first night he cooked for me, I got violently ill. I was hallucinating. Throwing up all the time. When I woke the next day I was out here in the woods. Somehow he had carried me here. I went back to the house and he acted like nothing was wrong. That I must have wandered off. That I had just gotten drunk. But it wasn't that. He had put something in my food. I'm sure of it."

Maiko looks at the gooseberry bush.

"Are those berries OK to eat?"

"The berries are, yes. But not the plant they grow on. The leaves, the stems, birds won't go near them, they must be poisonous. I can't find out. I have no phone. All my things are still back in that house. He won't let me back."

"You've been wandering around here for days? Weeks?"

"Yes. Like a vagrant. Stealing food from houses. Drinking from a stream. When I saw the van approaching, I thought you and Jason would rescue me, but you didn't even recognize me. You drove right on."

"But where did Pete think you were?"

"I don't think he cared all that much. He just wanted me out of the way. He took my wallet, my phone."

"What about Melissa? She must be out of her mind with worry!"

"There's no way I can contact her. My guess is Pete spun her some story. He wanted to get you both here. That was his plan all along. To hurt you both. No one would ever find you out here. And I'm sure if he comes across me again ... he'll kill me for good this time."

"But why? What does he want?"

"He only ever wanted Jason, and that the two of them be together as a group. A partnership in every way. You stole from him, that's what he thinks, stole everything. And when I suggested going in a different direction, with you as the main attraction, it all got too much for him."

Genki plops right down on the forest floor, as if the telling of this has exhausted him even further. He hands the water bottle back to Maiko and tells her he knows of a stream where ... but she already knows this.

Should Genki tell of naked Pete standing at the door of the house waving a samurai sword and shouting wild proclamations into the night? Words Genki (as good as his English is) had no notion of – whatever maniacal ramblings were coming out of him, he could not fathom. The words sounded ancient, the kind of things a prophet would have shouted from a mountaintop in an old tale. Genki had scampered back into the night like a terrified shrew, and Pete had laughed, had stood there laughing, a monster or maniac. He had never seen anything like it. And the music manager had seen plenty lose their meagre minds on the mean streets of the capital.

Maiko is stewing over everything she has just been told.

How precarious was the position they were now in?

Could she go back there?

And what about Jason?

Was he in imminent danger too?

"Jason said Pete had a weird upbringing. Unstable," explains Genki. "That first night in the house, he told me some of the things his uncle had done. A lot of it involved experimental drug use. He told me about coming to Japan, how his own father, some kind of priest, had kicked him out when he discovered he was gay. Pete made it here, borrowing money from his uncle, started as a language teacher, but began to play live in bars, and at parties. He did DJ sets. Anything with music. When he spoke about all this he would sometimes go into this strange trance-like spell ... it was unnerving."

"I've seen it. Just before. We need to get to the police. He needs to be stopped."

"But he hasn't done anything. What can we prove? Poison? How? Any poison I ingested is probably gone. I have nothing. He's made it like I don't exist. Without phone or wallet ... what am I to do? I can't go back there."

"But Jason, he's alone and…"

"We have to play along. Whatever mad game all this is, we have to play along with him. We must make sure he thinks that all is going according to his plan. You have to inform Jason. But don't eat what he cooks. And when the time is right you both get in the van and drive away. Make sure that sword he's got is out of the way. He keeps it in a long box in the tatami room. I saw him with it, chasing me through the woods out of his mind on some drug. He has moments of complete insanity. And there are animal traps laid out, all over the place, you know the ones, steel jaws, I saw a fox caught in one of them. I don't know if Pete laid them or not. There's a gardening shed next to the house, it's full of tools: I've slept in there one or two of the nights. But if you don't stick to the main paths, those traps…"

Maiko is trembling, the more he speaks the more she shakes.

It could not be true, any of it, could it?

"I'm not sure if I can do this."

"You have to. You have to get the three of us out of here. If he continues with his plans, he'll kill us all. He wants revenge… revenge for everything. It's been taken from him. His lover. His music. His sense of… purpose."

"So it's true about Jason and him. They did… they used to be *close*."

"That's what was taken from him."

"That's what *I took*."

"You must be careful, angel. Everything we do from now on must be done with utter care. But we can get out of this. Just play along. Just play his game."

Maiko crouches down to the man, hugs him and laughs nervously.

"You need to wash. I can get you some soap. But food is the priority. You look weak. You need to come to the kitchen window. When Pete is not looking I will throw out some food to you."

Like an animal, he thinks. Like a backyard dog.

She looks at him with pity.

"It's OK," he says. "This nightmare is going to end. We can get through this. We can win."

He holds her thin fingers in his own filthy hands and looks deeply into her liquid eyes.

"We will leave tonight. The three of us. When he's asleep. You have to make sure you have the keys of the van. Tell Jason the plan. We can do this. But please, please be careful … and play along. Play to his tune."

In her dreams … bears. She shouldn't ever watch the news on TV, the stories invade her dreaming, and if she isn't moaning, she is screaming.

The news had it that there were spates of attacks from bears in several prefectures around the country. A reporter had said that there was less food to eat in the mountains and they were coming down into the villages. Four had been injured in attacks in weeks previous, and such attacks were only to become more commonplace.

The bears load up on acorns before the winter. Maiko had laughed when she'd heard that. Acorns! She thought it was the food of squirrels. But the experts said they were highly calorific, highly nutritious, ideal food before their long slumber. A shortage of acorns was driving the bears into the villages, they were insane with hunger, their seasons out of joint.

The most horrific attacks came to be known as the Sankebetsu Incident in Hokkaido in 1915. Seven villagers were killed and three injured in a mauling by a huge brown bear, the likes no one had ever seen before. The TV reporter said the smaller Asian brown bear was the one that was hungry on the mainland, and that even though slighter in stature, was equally ferocious, that anything hungry could be that way.

Maiko moans when she sees herself chased by a rampaging bear through the panicked paths of her nightmares (how sweeter are the moans of Sayuri dreams: compassionate touches and the innocence of flesh … *not* the savaging of it).

Maiko often wakes from her dreams in sweat. So many things – summer, sex, savagery – making her sweat.
Is that a scent that can be picked up by other animals?
The stink of her own sweat?

21

The house says: I should fart you all out the door, let you fend for yourself, see how you fare, you lost children in the wilderness, if you dare.

A house can get sick, sick of what festers inside it.
A house does not want to die from this.

22

Maiko arrives at the house, breathless and bathed in perspiration. Was her scent picked up ... hungry hidden sniffing things in the forest pert and alert to it.

She is bent over, gasping; she is taking a minute to recoup.

She looks at the sofa that has been put there, outside, foolish in its incongruity. It is as if the house has spat it out, ridding itself of foul things, it needs no clutter. It could very well spit more, out of the house, item by item, piece by piece, until it is an empty shell.

This is what she will do with her music. She will spit, spit it all out, until she is an empty shell, spit spit spit – her period is definitely coming, cramps now, low down in her, makes her want to double up and cry from being born this way, woman, the clasp of the calendar, and the heat not helping matters. Sweat. Stink.

But she has to keep moving; other things are at stake. The word flashes across her mind: *stake*, a word learned, *at stake* ... and Joan of Arc was burned at ... and this word is spelled differently from *steak*. Homophones. Homos. What? She takes one more deep breath before stepping up to the house.

She sees the *welcome* mat, and wonders: really? *Welcome?* Really? Are any of them?

Her bandmates are practising and she follows the sounds into the main room. There they are. Music. Like nothing at all is amiss. *At stake?* Nothing: only the art of creation.

What do they know?

These are men. They sail through life easily. Month to month. Season to season.

Pete is at the synthesizer with his headphones on.

Jason has his guitar on his lap and rises when he sees his girl arrive, everything gets put aside and his smile is wide.

"What took so long?"

She checks to see that Pete is not eavesdropping, but he seems engrossed in his creation, has not even looked up to acknowledge her arrival. Does she actually exist or is she a phantom … no, the cramps make her real all right, corporeality, and the hellish nature of it.

She pulls him close to her, whispering, "Come upstairs in a few minutes. I need to tell you something."

She smiles at him falsely, if Pete looks up he would only catch fakery.

Maiko plants a tame kiss on Jason's cheek and then moves towards the band leader.

Pete responds to the approach by taking off his headphones, it's the least he can do.

She cannot gauge his look.

What is that … tension?

Authority?

Is that … ?

It's nothing at all.

Blank.

Dead behind the eyes.

His soul elsewhere.

"I just got a bit lost on the way back. I'm going to have a quick shower and then I promise I'll be ready."

She smiles again, even more falsely, does he pick that up? A woman's play … what men purchase …

He's swayed. Pete nods his permission, and she brushes his hand softly, trying to give the impression that nothing bad has ever passed between them, how could it have? A million years ago. It was all a million years ago. Things always move on. Only onwards. She should go. She should leave him now, but she stays a moment longer.

"Thank you for this morning. The gooseberries. Amazing. I actually ate some more of them. I think I can get used to the taste and texture."

She is smiling so much that Jason thinks she must be on something. High. Had they found mushrooms? Gotten high without him knowing it? That's unfair.

"We're going to have a great afternoon session. I can feel it. We're going to make some great music."

Pete smiles weakly, unsure of her, unsure even of his own reaction to her. But he is inclined to believe what she says. Men purchase.

Jason doesn't know what to think, doesn't know what instrument to pick up, doesn't know what has happened this morning, doesn't know why they are where they are, doesn't know what beast took the food, doesn't know why the welcome mat got turned around the other way, why there is a couch outside and not inside, doesn't know what day it even is, and where the sword happens to be, that weapon, dried blood on its tip, and what did she mean: *I have to tell you something*.

Maiko leaves the music room.

Melancholy music, after a minute, resumes. Some people just live to create.

23

She stands in the hallway, her back to the wall, and tries to settle herself.

Endure, she tells herself. Endure.

Life was not meant to be enjoyed, no, not at all. Pete had said that to her once. He was referencing Schopenhauer again. Not enjoyed, *endured*. It stuck. Pete's words stick. His notions.

He is often in her head. How quickly people can creep inside, like a beaver with sticks building a set, diverting the course of a river.

And he was in that room now, playing melancholy sounds, as if nothing at all had happened, as if nothing.

Had it?
Had something happened?
A slap.
That was all.
Everyone gets a slap every now and again. It did no one any harm, did it? Put you in your place. Where is your place?

Settle.

But how can you settle when your insides are churning and your mind, never for one second, stops its brutal turning?

Maiko moaned and her mother knew. It was her time. It had come. Maiko and her mother from that moment on shared a secret joke (it was about all they ever shared and ever lasted): *The aliens from outer space.*

It was a way of talking about it without adjacent men knowing (they hardly cared, hardly ever listened, unless it was something to do with the readiness of lunch or dinner and how soon it would appear on the table, for their eyes and for their bellies to feast, the beasts).

The aliens from outer space have come.

Or: *the aliens from outer space have landed on our planet.*

Well, then we'll just have to deal with them. They are unwelcome. They mean no harm, and yet, they have to be dealt with. They will not stay long.

There were hot pads you could lay across the stomach, for relief. There were pills to help with the pain. But always, you needed to be ready. You did not actually need to see them flying over in their spaceships to know they would be arriving, visiting for a few days. They always sent clear signals.

Maiko and her mother. Was that all they shared?

Brief moment of womanhood. A passing down of wisdom.

An odd, secret way of talking: *Aliens from outer space.*

There was little else in the way of love, affection; it was the way of their people, people at work, jobs and the doing of things, jobs and being busy with things, little time for displays of emotion and affection – that was the stuff of daytime TV dramas, no one gave much credence, and everyone knew people were not actually like that, not really like that. Perhaps that's why she grew fond of fleeing. Perhaps that's why the prospect of foreigners, who were more inclined…

Not enjoyable, sure, life.

Endurable?

In the process of removing her clothes.

There isn't blood in her underwear yet, but soon: she needs to deal with that. Always having to deal with.

Preparations: the preparations of the female; the anticipation, the always being ready, the always being aware and being ready, that's what woman is – she might sing about it sometime, or maybe moan about it, or just spit spit spit till she's an empty shell.

The aliens from outer space.

The aliens from outer space.

A soft rap on the door.

"What the fuck is going on?"

Impatient. Impetuous. Man.

"Remember when we were driving here, and a man jumped out in front of the van?"

Jason is nodding.

"And you said that he looked like a homeless version of Genki."

"Yeah."

"Well, get this: it was Genki! It was actually him!"

"What?"

"Pete poisoned him."

"What the fuck?"

"And now he's out to harm both of us. This music plan … this new album, whatever. New songs. It's all bullshit. He wants rid of us all. Or at least rid of me. He's fucking insane, Jason. I can't go into all the details but … "

Jason reels from the onslaught of information. He has to sit on the side of the bathtub as she prepares to shower, prepares to prepare. He cannot even look at her and appreciate her beautiful form. His thoughts are too cyclonic. What had she said? Poisoned? *Poisoned?* None of this makes any sense. But then, it is Pete Illtyd she refers to, after all … so …

She can see the look of incredulity on his face and then that incredulity morphing into some kind of recognition. Yes, Jason knows Pete, knows him better than anyone else around here (and there is no one else around here).

"We have to play along. Whatever he says we do."

She is naked and she is stepping towards the shower and she is still talking and she is beautiful and he could get aroused were he thinking straight, but he is far from that.

"Whatever he says, we do. Let him rule. We rehearse this afternoon like there's nothing wrong. Like there's nothing to worry about. Our faces can't reveal the slightest bit of doubt."

Jason is pacing. A bobcat trapped. Claws are out but what can they scratch?

"We can't show him anything, Jason. Do you understand? We'll escape tonight."

"Escape? What do you mean *escape*...?"

"We're going to have to get the keys and...wait...do you hear something?"

The bottom of the stairs: Pete is looking up, ear cocked. Suspicious.

"You two all right up there? We're going to get started soon...this is no time for hanky-panky."

One of the strangest phrases she has ever heard, *hanky-panky*. But she has no time to consider it.

Jason takes her advice, tries not to show.

"Coming, Pete, buddy. Be right there."

Maiko is shaking her head. No, not *buddy*. Already that's too much. She's a woman, knows more about deception. Can talk about aliens when men are in the room and they're too tuned-out to take any notice, if it doesn't concern them, if there's nothing in it for them.

She runs the water of the shower. It looks so enticing, the gush. Scrub it off. All of it. Sweat. Dirt. Pete.

She steps in and under the water flow, still keeping her voice low, conspiratorial.

"Tonight, at dinner. He will cook. But no way are you to eat the green slices he gives you. It will look like asparagus or something. But we can't eat it."

"Are you fucking serious?"

"Shush. Keep your voice down. He's probably listening in. We can't let on. Just play along. That's what Genki said."

"Jesus Christ, this is fucking nuts. I mean, I knew the guy was weird but…did something happen in the forest? Did he try something?"

Maiko hesitates. She holds her face to the rush of the water. She does not look at her partner. Her lover.

"He slapped me."

Jason clenches. Ripples under tattoos.

"No. Don't. Don't get angry now, Jason. Now's not the time. We'll get out of all of this before…before it, before *he*, gets worse. He's not well. The important thing is that you, me, and Genki get out. Tonight. Before he loses it completely."

She's thinking of other English words and phrases: *imminent, on the cards, boiling point,* so much she has acquired, but she cannot say them all now. It is no time for discussion, just preparation. The always preparing. A woman's life. If she has been born for anything it is for moments like these.

"Why is he doing this?"

"Because…you and me. The way the music is going…a fucked-up past. Many reasons. But look, go, go…go play with him."

She is like a mother shooing her child out the door to engage with another on a clement day.

Bewildered, he leaves.

Pete is still at the bottom of the stairs and looking up at him.

"What's going on?"

"Nothing. Nothing. Hard to keep away from a beautiful woman, you know," Jason laughs weakly.

Pete scowls.

He stays completely still for another few seconds then begins to relax his demeanour ... a little.

How many people are inside him: Jason wonders.

Past.

Pasts?

All that philosophy he read, and the batshit religion, and the botany, and the music: who the fuck is he? And how did Jason ever get involved? Was he so desperate for friendship, friendship in a strange land where he didn't speak the language and clung to anyone who had the merest thing in common? Was he that desperate? *In common?* Just the music. No. Not *buddy*. Definitely not. Maiko's right.

"Just going to get us some cold coffee cans from the fridge."

Jason scurries past him and heads to the kitchen, a big man but with such small movements again.

The air of the refrigerator is refreshing when it is opened and hits his flushed face.

24

Pete Illtyd is on a laptop and is playing ambient music which pours aural lava out from large speakers – is this the new direction? Is this where he wants to take them? Ambient? New directions? Or is it to appease the scratchy voices in his head? Scratching: Scripture, uncles, gooseberries in the forest, what lies beneath, buried.

Jason arrives with two cold cans of coffee and he hands one over to the band leader. He is nodding along with the surrounding sound, the series of waves, bereft of any beat, waves, yes, waves, as if he can picture himself surfing on their crests and undulations: American-thinking, surfer dude, hang ten, even from a Montana boy.

"Under the gooseberry bush."

"What?"

"The name of this track."

"Right. Yeah. No. Cool."

Jason sips from the can. He rarely praises his partner on anything these days. Is *cool* enough? Do people still say that? What is this shit?

Pete persists, peculiar in his thoughts, "Roots. Fertilizer. Things decaying and providing nutrition for other things."

Jason is unsure. He is thinking of how when he was young he would love to pore over the inlay cards on cassette tapes, or the information inside CD jackets, where they explained what the music was about, or where the lyrics were displayed. Sometimes songwriters would pen their own explanations: sometimes that tactic worked, sometimes it was pure gibberish. Imagine if someone picked up Pete's explanations. *Roots. Fertilizer. Things decaying and providing nutrition for other things.* It would make little sense to anyone. Music listeners don't have to read anymore, things are downloaded, existing on a different plane, nothing physical about any of it, Pete can't bring anything physical into the world, just these tamperings with air vibrations that reach ears – if those ears are receptive … and who on earth will be?

Still, he praises again, keeping the peace, acting like there's nothing wrong and Maiko hasn't told him anything.

Nothing happened out there in the forest.

Nothing at all.

"Yeah. Nice. I like it. Really."

"Needs more bass."

"Sure."

"And I don't want the guitar to come in until later: let it build for a minute first. And if there is guitar to be on it, then it should be like … William Tyler-ish … wispier. Or else we erase it completely. Give it more space."

"Got it."

"More space. Yeah, lots of space."

"Sure."

The playback continues. It fills the room. The white room. Black curtains. And they fill it too. The room. Space. Both of them. Their hands holding little coffee cans … as if they are grenades.

The leader must stay leader.

"You not going to the magic box then?"

"Nah, I thought I'd keep a clear head. Wanna get this right. Our music. And I want to get back to the city … impress Genki."

Subtle. A gentle probe.

"Haven't heard from him, have you? Genki?"

"Phones not working up here. You know that."

"But on the computer there."

"No Wi-Fi. Nothing here. Just us. And our challenges."

Pete refuses eye-contact all this time, as if the sounds are all he is interested in. The waves, the waves continue, rising, falling, strange they are, like liquid but filling the air, or those elements combining.

It does sound good, all of this. Pete is proud.

And if Jason is honest, the more he listens, the more it grows on him.

"Genki's probably just leaving us at it then. Giving us some space. You know what I mean?"

"Yeah, probably."

Jason starts rubbing his head and Pete notices.

"What's wrong with you?"

"Headache coming on."

"Hangover."

"No, the weather. It feels like it's going to pour. Thunderstorm. Can't you feel it? The tension?"

Pete stares at the black curtain while focusing again on the sounds he created.

"No. I feel nothing."

His fingers move on the computer keyboard – things move accordingly on the computer screen.

"Right."

Jason may as well join in. Do what he's supposed to do. He picks up an electric guitar and starts to play a little.

Can he add to this? He fiddles with pedals on the floor. There's a wah-wah. What the hell is that doing here? This day and age. When was the last time a wah-wah excited anyone? "Fool's Gold"? Jesus Christ, years ago. He fiddles more. Adjusts levels.

Maiko comes in, showered, refreshed, the dirt off of her at last. The forest outside is outside, none of it is on her. She's wearing a bra inside her T-shirt this time, and she has jeans on. She's covered.

"It's going to rain," she says.

"That's what I just said to Pete. Thunder on the way."

Nothing but practice then, practice for being a band, together, practice for sounds and what they can achieve; it's done with such focus, gets them all out of themselves for a while, the focus is everything, intent, the music, what they can create, give a little here, let go there, make your point, argue your case, but there is no vindictiveness while any of this is happening, tension sure, but not of the dangerous kind, nothing explosive, no grenades really, they are just coffee cans, and Jason tries not to think about what Maiko said and Maiko tries not to think about what she had told him, but moans instead, the beginning of some kind of lyrics, embryonic yet, just rumblings, practice, practice is all, and Pete keeps uncles and books and philosophy and scripture and all those things out of his head, nothing along those lines, just bass instead, and guitar, and computer ambience, and synthesizer sounds, and the speakers hum and hiss and crackle occasionally and feedback sometimes too, from the speakers and from their mouths, and dud notes and wrong chords and stumbles and falls, but that's what it means to be in a band, and for a brief while they are that, a band, as if nothing could go wrong, as if all is fine and nothing bad would ever happen and none of them would lose their way.

Sometimes her moans are of pleasure, more often than not: this is the case.

But sometimes they are fake: necessary, to end it, to not let it proceed any further, enough is enough.

Sometimes she does things out of duty, not questioning why.

Sometimes they are to get out of a mess she shouldn't have gotten herself into in the first place, a misstep. Pretence. That's it: fakery.

Fake moans.

Did you?

Of course.

You sure?

Of course. I wouldn't lie to you.

Do you want to try again ... another?

No, I'm tired now. But really, I did, it was great.

One sleeps, sated, snores, the other, it takes a while, a little guilt.

But it is necessary sometimes, to get out of what you shouldn't have gotten yourself into in the first place ... like it's some kind of breach of contract ... but how would he ever know?

25

The house says nothing.
The house is listening in. Accepts the harmony. A hiatus.
But for how long?
How long such harmony?
How long the hiatus?
The house doubts.

26

Genki is walking in the woods, a wild man. He is approaching the house and approaching warily.

He stops when he thinks he hears growls. It could be his own paranoia. It could be something that wants to kill him. It could be his own stomach folding in on itself out of dire need.

He trots further. Towards. Sticks to the narrow path, not in amongst the trees where you never know what can leap out at you, never know where the jaws are hidden and ready to sink their mechanical teeth into your skinny limbs. One misstep. All it takes.

Suddenly thunder and suddenly downpour. Lightning across the sky to add to the meteorological drama, as if he is not pathetic enough, he is wet now, soon to be soaked right through. This is the closest he can get to washing, letting nature rid him of his stink, or will it only add to his putrescence?

He hurries to the gardening toolshed near the back of the house, opens the door quietly and slips in. He keeps the door slightly ajar and has a view of the house and its kitchen window. He stares out hungrily, knowing what kitchens contain, imagines stocked shelves, cupboards, fridges, freezers. Would that it were a house of gingerbread and he could run and launch himself widely and widely gnaw into its very façade.

27

"Pretty good."

"You look surprised, Pete. Didn't think we had it in us, did you? And only on our second day."

Pete half-smiles at her, "I thought your heads weren't in it."

"Like I said, we just needed time to settle."

Thunder roars.

Wind howls.

If they could only record it, add that to their new direction, ambience, found sounds. Brewing storms.

"I knew that was coming, all morning. Fucking headache."

"You're so in tune with nature here. Maybe you do belong here after all."

Jason playfully gives Maiko the finger. He once told her it was *flipping the bird.* She asked about the origin, the etymology, he said he didn't know, shrugged. Just: *the bird.*

Pete watches them. He wants none of this banter. Business is all.

"We need to eat something. I'll fix us up something for dinner."

He leaves them, and their fake smiles fall to seriousness and to sighs of relief, shoulders drop from strain.

Maiko immediately starts searching around the room.

"What are you looking for?"

"The keys. To the van."

"Shit, yeah. I don't know where they are."

"I think he's got them. They must be in his bag."

Maiko is impatient, "Where's his fucking bag?"

"I don't know. His room, I guess. I'll go check it out. If he comes, shout for me. Make an excuse."

They hug before he goes, an adventure; this is an adventure now, not what they had expected from their sojourn. They had come to make music, to lay down new tracks, eke out a new musical direction, band, bond, band-bond together, now they had only thoughts of escape.

Escape?

From what?

To what?

What lunacy was all this?

Mere paranoia?

Or where they seriously in danger?

The creative minds, tendencies to exaggerate, simply thinking often got the better of them. Not a moment's peace. Pete was just an ordinary dude, right? A little lost, maybe. Sure. Little weird maybe. Yeah.

But they couldn't take any chances, right?

The room is sparsely decorated.

His rucksack is beside the folded-up futon on the floor, and quickly Jason's hands plunge in, diving to depths as if for pearl.

Nothing substantial though. Nothing special, nothing metal, nothing that jangles, fail.

One credenza at the side of the room has small, dainty drawers; it's made out of some kind of black lacquer, typically Japanese, typically alien to an American more used to sycamore, red and sugar maple, things carved out of quaking aspen, ponderosa (he is an imposter, this room, this land) … but he goes to the tall construction.

The first few drawers have nothing but random pizza and *bento* takeaway leaflets (where on earth could those establishments be? They are so far out here, so far away in the country) coupon cut-out flyers, all expired, all useless.

But in the bottom drawer he takes out a collection of four or five old fading photographs.

Polaroids.

These are not what he is after, but they are a find nonetheless.

One picture shows a younger Pete – the hairline was present then and not retreating like a cowardly infantry line – his arm slung around the shoulder of a similarly-aged, scrawny, effeminate wisp of a human, the kind of effete being Jason knew stocky Pete could burden and govern. Groom.

He turns the picture over. On its smooth white reverse, etched with what must have been a hard-pushed, deliberate pen: "Peter and Haruki: true love."

There is no date.

Jason's eyes are wide and welcoming and he skips quickly through the others. Haruki is nude and holding the sword in one of them – it could be a pastiche pose of writer and insurgent Yukio Mishima, complete with white headband, but there is no look of fierceness on this face, clearly having too much fun to maintain the make-believe. It is of course the same sword; the one Jason was so careless with; *You could have fucking killed me!*

Jason takes out his phone and takes snapshots of these old snapshots. These will be useful somehow, if not for bribery or evidence, then at least to show to Maiko, for a gasping gossip if nothing else, for when they are both away in the van, away to easeful elsewhere, sitting safe and cool in some air-conditioned café and drinking iced-coffee and wondering what it had all been about.

Pete and Haruki? Who the fuck? True love. What?

But they are not in that cool, air-conditioned café yet.

A creak on the wooden stairs.

Footsteps outside the door.

An approach.

Jason's heart bangs, a bass drum inside of him.

Shit.

He holds himself very still, hardly breathes, the photographs still in his hand now trembling. His blood thrums, pulsing there, a vein at his temple.

The door opens.

Maiko.

Phew, Jesus Christ: the exhalation of relief comes right from his quivering diaphragm.

"C'mon back down. I've already found them. The keys."

"Where were they?"

"In his guitar case all along. Buried under sets of spare strings."

"Buried, sure."

So much around here. Covered over. He can't wait to tell her just what he's just found.

Matrimonial moans.

He once mentioned marriage. Maiko nearly spat out the tea that she'd been drinking.

Seriously?

Perhaps Jason hadn't been serious, but he had gone ahead and said it all the same. After beer, copious, of course. Drunk again. Quick to remove his T-shirt and show his pecks and his tats and for her to try and resist (she did). It was so much easier to say things when you were *sozzled* (a Pete word), she got to know this, these patterns of behaviour. *Dutch courage* was one name for it. Pete taught her that phrase, too.

It shouldn't have been so funny: marriage. But it was. She couldn't help but think of it as a kind of joke, a cruel one. She had her own parents' example. The neglected children; not poor, not hungry, just the lack of hugs (is this what pushed her to drugs, or is that too cosy a line of inquiry?), what anyone of them would have done for a pat on the head, a compliment on a good drawing that could have been pinned to the refrigerator door. A cliché. That's what she wanted. But those kinds of things didn't materialise. Marriage? Seriously? Family? Fuck me. They couldn't even keep a band together without quarrel or quandary, even those who had the same interests, the same compulsions to create – what hope was there?

Jason also had asked that evening if her father would be happy to *give her away*. It was another phrase she had to soak up and keep, and how odd, *give away*. Just like that. Off you go. I am giving you away. I no longer want you, no longer need you. I have no use for you. Or, I never really needed you in the first place. You just arrived and we got stuck with you, and then more, just like you. Girls. Boys. Whatever. They had their jobs, their own things to do: parents, guardians. Everybody's got their own shit to be getting on with. Maiko heard foreign people complain about the coldness of the people in Japan, and how the busy-ness of life actually suited their collective personality: they didn't have to be loving to others, better the distances, the keep-aways, aloofness – it was a harsh summation, it was probably completely erroneous, this stereotype, but Maiko didn't mind it at all. It tallied her life quite accurately. She'd rather be busy being creative, as long as those creative things were worthwhile, praiseworthy. Worth. Worth. (You had to get your pronunciation right on that one, so as not to say *worse*. They sounded so similar to her Japanese ears. Language: a tricky business. Second languages: trickier.)

Marriage? She had spat.

And then she said what she was so getting used to saying to him, and had no trouble pronouncing: *Go fuck yourself.*

28

"No, you two relax, enjoy the honeymoon."

Maiko grimaces.

Both she and Jason are sitting at the kitchen table, like he has told them to do. They are watching him at the sink, washing vegetables, preparing food. He said he wanted no help. Absolutely not. He wanted to do everything by himself. Solo.

It's getting darker outside the curtainless kitchen window. Not full-on night yet, but the moon has made an appearance and then went and got itself hidden again behind hurrying carts of clouds and their freight of heavy rains.

Rivulets down the pane and thunder still intermittently sounding in the sky: Jason is Americanly aware that it could be the soundtrack or set-up to a Scream scenario, the movie pawns all in place… but it couldn't be all that obvious, could it? Pete as madman? Still, his insides pulse with possibilities, outcomes; there is simply so much he doesn't know about him, his *leader*. And then again there is so much he *does*.

Fuck. He does. He does know.

Turns and turns, flips and flips, his stomach, and not just from hunger.

Those photographs – how much does anyone know about anyone? If all you know of these people is the result of a hobby – which is all it is really, when you get down to it: a hobby, music, an escape from real work, isn't it, isn't that all it really is?

Work is what their fathers and mothers do. The making of money. Earning. Livings. The real world. Real people. As Jason has so often been reminded. How patronising it was to hear it. And they still say it. Facetimes and Zooms. Perpetually reminded. The real world. Not some ivory tower. His extended holiday. How long has he been there now? How long? And what to show for it all? Was he ever thinking of coming home? What keeps him there? They joke in Montana that he will come home with a Japanese wife. Now wouldn't that be something? No doubt she'd be a stunner. Or cute as a button. Petite. Jet black hair. Radiant eyes. But he never mentions girls. He says he has been on a few dates, but he's been busy. Keeping busy at work, always. Work is crazy here, non-stop – what a work-ethic these people have. They think he's a language teacher. They do not know that he has put all his eggs in the music basket, and now the music basket might have a false bottom.

A joke. What a joke.

LCD Soundsystem plays on the CD player and Pete, as he cuts and slices, rants on about the great YouTube clip of the band preparing for their farewell concert – before they actually reunited, and what was all that about, to quit and then be at it again – and Murphy and his team alighting the stage and "Dance Yrself Clean" starts up, and it's a full five minutes before that beat drops and when it does, mate, when it does, it never fails to put a shiver up the spine. It is the greatest beat-drop in all of musical history according to Pete. And worth the wait. Like all things. The best things in life. The best things in life are worth the wait. Pete is adamant about this. Is being so forthright. And the two bandmates just listen to him, his patter, his chatter, and of course they are not really listening to him at all, it's just that they have their faces turned towards him, turned but not tuned in to anything he has to say, who cares, it's all like static, all white noise, the blood in their ears, and his knife, Pete's knife, sharp and reflecting the harsh light of the shadeless bulb, no, not *really* listening, not tuned in to his waffle, who gives a shit what Pete thinks about LCD Soundsystem or any old band or any other old matter, he has the knife in his hand, and Maiko can see him clearly slicing the greens that he took from the transparent plastic bag on the counter just now, as he works, cuts and slices, and she knows what they are. Those are the gooseberry stems. Or stalks. Or whatever they are called – she's a country girl but she's not a what…a botanist. The plant they grow on, a gooseberry bush. Her own two eyes, saw it…before she got slapped. *The leaves, the stems, birds won't go near them, they must be poisonous.* He had cut them off that morning. She remembers that much. How could she forget? And here he is preparing them now. For their pleasure. Or at least for his.

"Looking forward to this, Pete. Haven't eaten all day. So wrapped up in the music. Starving."

Through his teeth, Jason, lying.

Maiko is nodding.

Pete is not turning around to look at them, stays busy with his chores. Then Jason tries something, out of bravery, or foolishness:

"Genki will be delighted. With the music, I mean. With our productivity. Can't wait for him to hear it."

Pete stiffens at the kitchen sink. Stops. The knife is in his hand. He still doesn't turn to them. He can see their reflection in the window. They have their eyes on his back, like burning holes. All three of them are stiff now.

Thunder again.

Sparks of electricity lighting up the night sky, darker now, and Pete sees the wind pull open the back door of the toolshed; it's swinging there on its hinges and making a banging sound, loud, rhythmic. Better than they could make. He frowns.

"Jay? Do you mind going out and having a look at that shed. That door shouldn't be open."

"Sure…but…"

"But…what?"

"Like if there's…"

"No bear will come this close to the house, not in a thunderstorm. It's probably just a fox or a raccoon dog or something, sheltering from the inclemency."

Pete turns and looks at them both, flashes a smile.

"That's a nice word, isn't it? *Inclemency.*"

Maiko smiles. She doesn't know what it means. She's never heard the word. She doesn't know the meaning of Pete either. Who is he and why is he here, and why has she gotten herself into a situation where she is in a strange kitchen – who even owns this fucking place? – and he is cooking for her, and what he cooks might just kill her. The whole premise is absurd. It's ludicrous. And yet here she is and here she sits. She had pitied him. For months she had pitied him. He looked so ugly next to her handsome American. It was cruel, the way she thought of him. Pete: ugly. A cruel way to think. Like features mattered. Like anything does. But she is wondering now who will have the last laugh. And who in the kitchen is the one holding the sharp knife. Who is in control?

Thunder, more: must be close.

Maiko feels pain in her lower abdomen. Yes, sure. Her time, coming. Or it's here already. Stress only accelerates. Often conceived of as imminent … and it's there already, before you know it, manifested, spots on undergarments. She needs to check.

"If you'll excuse me, I … "

She has never sounded so polite to them before. Why now? Nerves? This is not the place she wants to be. She wants to be in a loud music venue with the only cacophony being the thunder coming from a bass guitar and its massive amplifiers, vibrating floors, bone-shaking – that's what she wants. Maybe some dark singer is screaming into a microphone, screaming about confusion and pain and the pointlessness of life – that's what she wants, that's all. The clever people could have their philosophy books and the stupid people could have their religions, but all she needed was a screamer at the microphone explaining how life really is: savage and sore and unfair and blood seeping out of you once a month. Perhaps, she thinks, as she mounts the creaking stairs, perhaps she'd be better off in Norway or Sweden or wherever they had those dark metal bands, bands with names like Darkthrone, Mayhem, Satyricon, that roared their pains and bawled like they were in cahoots with the guardians of the pits of hot hurting hell. For hell exists. And they are never far from it, these humans. Ask any woman alone with two men in a lonesome, stifling country place, and when one of them has a knife and seems unafraid to use it...

Creak.

Up the stairs she goes to check on herself. Emissions for sure. Menses. The calendar. At least it was dependable. She wondered about men, what made the calendar present for them, or was it some ephemeral thing, nebulous, just one week striding into the next without any demarcation at all.

She remembers the first time a boy had taken her behind a shed – yes, sheds again, becoming emblematic for her; the one outside has a door that keeps banging.

And he wanted to touch her there, in her private parts. He was some greasy country boy who never seemed to wash his hair. He smelled, and when he tried to smile he only made things worse, the flecks of green lodged between his teeth, cankers on the inside of lips. She didn't want herself anywhere near him. She was a year or so older than him and clearly of more clout, so she was able to bargain: she would of course show him her *thing*, if only he showed his thing first. The poor boy, naturally he succumbed. Taken in. Fooled. He was a male and so it was easy, and it would probably happen many more times in his life. And she looked down and saw it, and again it was an occasion in her life when she was forced to cover her mouth so as not to rudely laugh. That was what the fuss was all about? That little slug of a thing? She didn't know then that it would be capable of doing so much damage, if provoked, should some more accommodating country girl ever get beyond the reek of the lad who would one day become a man, and allow him access. But Maiko was not to be that girl. Instead of showing him her private thing, she just ran off, leaving him there with his pathetic slug out and his dirty jeans around his ankles. It was a lesson for him, she thought. Don't be so quick to make a bargain, especially with those older and faster than you. And wiser. Wiser.

She moans as she cleans herself, getting sanitary napkins from her bedroom and slipping on fresh underwear.

She moves to the bedroom window and tries to see out, tries to see the unfortunate wretch who might be cowering in that shed, cold and wet and scared, her Genki.

But the rain beats too hard against the pane and the darkness is too massive with itself and she only sees herself and her own darkness and has to abandon the notion.

"Don't worry, sweetheart," she says to the empty room. "We'll get you, we'll get you out of here."

She likes *sweetheart*. No one ever said any such things to her in her life: *princess, darling, honey*. A dearth of endearments. Sad, really. Awfully sad. Genki sometimes calls her *angel* and she almost melts every time.

In the kitchen Pete stops his chopping.

He goes to Jason who has not moved from the chair.

"I thought you were going to go and check on the toolshed. Lock up the door."

"Yeah, but … "

"Yeah, but what, big man … you a pussy?"

Jason doesn't move. The blood beats at his temple again.

Pete pulls the knife on him, whip-fast, holds it close to that throbbing temple so that the point is pressed to the bulge of vein.

Pete is smiling.

"If the animal comes at you, whatever it is, you just put the blade to its throat like I've just done … see … then … when you are ready, you push it in, and twist."

Jason gulps.

"You got that?"

"Pete, look, you're acting kinda crazy, man, put away the fucking knife."

"Oh crazy, am I? Was I the one walking around with a sword this morning, playing at being a samurai? Like I said, my *buddy*, my big *man-pussy-buddy*, if you are to hold something like this in your hand, you have to be prepared to use it. Don't you agree?"

Jason nods. Sweat on his brow. And fine hairs rising at the back of his neck – is that fear, or excitement? How fucked up are they, the whole lot of them?

"I'm going to go and check on the toolshed."

Pete pulls the knife way from Jason's head.

"Great. A big lad like you has nothing to be afraid of."

Jason stands, he towers over the small man, but at that moment, which one of them seems bigger?

Pete turns the knife around in his hand and offers it to Jason, handle first, the blade flat on his own palm.

"Go on, take it. You can either go out and see what the matter is, or, you can thrust it into me right now, any part of me you wish. Penetrate."

Pete's eyes are wider than Jason has ever seen them before.

"Go on, don't be scared. Big man like you. Thrust it. I remember when you thrust into me before."

He hums a few notes of The Stooges' "Penetration".

Jason takes the knife, his hand trembling.

"There there, no need to be nervous. We're all a bit *high tension* tonight. Maybe we should have dinner and relax and have a drink and forget about all this … stress. We've had a good day of music. Shouldn't we be celebrating?"

He is grinning now and Jason turns away from his leer. He heads into the hallway and then out the main door, out to greet the weather, to meet the dark night, to meet whatever might be lurking in that toolshed.

He circles around the house and goes to the toolshed. His heart is in tandem with the night's tumult and his face feels hot, even in the assuaging rain. He is soaked in seconds. The heat and humidity of the place seem to have vanished, cleared by this monstrous downpouring. He could nearly shiver, as if a new season had suddenly begun and enveloped the place – or it could be the fright inside him, shocking his nerves, the fright of the night and all that he has witnessed in the last few minutes. What was wrong with that cunt?

Jason's thoughts echo that of his lover's: why is he here and why has he gotten himself into a situation where he is in a lonesome house, their leader (leader!) cooking some crap for him and growing further deranged and … it seems absurd. It is. The whole fucking thing. Each thing he considers. And yet it is all happening.

He stands outside the toolshed.

He'll have to go in.

29

A *right moan.*
  Pete.

He had even taught this phrase to Maiko. His subordinate. Maybe Maiko learned to do it all by herself, it was what humans did, never happy with their lot, needed exterminating really, like vermin, the whole sodding race. *With him is the strength and wisdom: the deceived and the deceiver are his.* They are now. His. There for the taking.

Pete moans about the past and the present. The way things are now is not how he wants things to be. His orders shouldn't be disobeyed like that. They don't do what he says. Or they do so but do so reluctantly. It is not good enough.

His father. His father had orders and they were never disobeyed. Lest the lash. But Father left. Pete moans about his father. Big-bearded, a hulk of a man. A mountain. And when Pete was naughty, the nearest weapon was brought out, a belt loosed from the band of his trousers, or a walking stick, a shillelagh (a gift from an Irish traveller, he remembers), whipped across the back of the thighs. Pete had assumed that violence was a normal part of everybody's upbringing. His father then absconded, with his Bible and his booze. It was hard to know which of those was more important to the old geezer, which of them helped him breathe more fire. It seemed he needed both. Consumed both with utter conviction, dedication. Spewed them both back out. Wretched stuff that filled the boy's life; rooms that stank of puke, and Bible quotations that hung on every wall, fake parchments, bad art, poorly executed thrift-store tapestries: Old Testament, New Testament, it didn't matter. It was all there to be rammed down the throat of an innocent, someone clueless enough not to know what's what, weak enough to never mount an insurrection. Pete thought that all Welsh families were like that, until he visited other houses of other people, saw that they weren't like that at all. Were very different indeed. He saw with his own astonished eyes that they didn't give a shit about the Bible or didn't even have a copy in the house. Pictures on the walls were of haystacks, or photographs of weddings, of graduations, football heroes. And their houses never smelled of vomit and piss. That was the revelation, far greater than the ones Pete had been forced to read in those musty, thin-papered old books.

Finally, his father left. Against all this teaching, all his lessons of morality, he vanished, a puff of smoke, a trick of Lucifer then and not some God after all, a dastardly devil departed. His two things, Bible and bottle of stout, one in each hand, and eyes demented and longing for a road, any road to any other old place that would put up with his shit before they too cottoned on to him; the fact that most losers just stay lost; that he had lost his wife somewhere along that lost highway too … and where did she go?

Lost lost lost.

Peter never solved that one. He's searching still. His mother. Some said the loony bin. Some said the bottom of Mywngil. *Some say the devil is dead. More say he rose again.* That was a song he'd heard: the old Irish banjo-picking traveller with his lice-infested mane and a nose like rotting, flea-flecked fruit.

He'd heard a lot, Pete, was quick to learn songs and rhymes, to keep them all ringing in his head. To even make stabs at his own.

Uncle taught him to play the fiddle.
Uncle taught him about Schopenhauer, Kierkegaard, Hegel.
Uncle taught him the box accordion, a few notes on the piano.

He learned to play the guitar himself, an old one that had been abandoned, left in a rubbish tip, and he had polished it up, stole a packet of strings from Mulvane's Music store on the high street and strung it himself, badly, but strung it, and learned to play it himself – there was a pop song out at the time about a fella playing it till his *fingers bled*. That was what Pete Illtyd did. Blood came out the tips of his fingers until eventually calluses formed.

And Uncle grew stuff. Vegetables. Fruits that could stand the soil and the scarcity of sun and bulge into something edible. And mysterious leaves in wardrobes that needed special lights that when harvested could be rolled into cigarettes along with the tobacco and could be smoked. It hurt the lungs first, but you sort of got used to it. The same way you got used to philosophical rants, daft diatribes against the establishment, dismantling of ideologies – whatever those things were – the smell of hippies coming to stay and cooing like old pigeons around the place, their putrid patchouli all over the house as bad as his father's old vomit that stained the carpet and never really left, marks of fetid demons, indelible.

And folk songs.

Rebel songs from people who weren't really that rebellious at all, who just wanted easier ways and not to strive for anything.

And tablets that dissolved on your tongue and took you to places that you never knew were inside your own head, undiscovered countries there, undiscovered galaxies.

Pete moans at the memories of them all, the people, their wares.

And Hendrix and Cream.

And Bitches Brew.

And Janis Joplin and Joe Cocker.

Faust.

And Ornette Coleman that welded well with the stuff he smoked or ingested, the mad meanderings of tune and thought, gelling, pushing each other along on strange currents that wended their way, and he rode atop them, carried along, roads to God knows where.

He was only a kid.

Uncle called it an education. A better one than he'd ever get at those conventional comprehensive schools. But even as a child he had his doubts. There was unconventionality, and then there was downright madness. But he managed to stay in classrooms long enough to get the results he needed, and enough to study botany in Aberystwyth, enough to get there at least. That was the first step. And when that was done, after lonely years of no girls and nothing but music and more drugs and experimentation with an increasingly senile uncle, he saw an advertisement in the newspaper that was looking for young people to teach the English language in Japan. That couldn't be too hard, could it? And it would be something new. A fresh start. Maybe he could leave the drugs and the memories behind. A clean break. His uncle and the unwashed women that lay around his living room floor stinking the place and playing daft folk songs in warblingly annoying voices, memories of those would surely all vanish the same way his father did. Puff. Smoke. Begone with ye.

Surely surely surely, he could order his cause. Declare himself to ears that would listen.

Yes, vanish.

Another land.

Rebirth.

As the cloud is consumed and vanisheth away: so he that goeth down to the grave shall come up no more.

Down to the grave?

Things are buried around here.

Things are buried everywhere.

The soil, nothing but the memories it contains.

Here he is moaning now: Pete moans.

Often when they are at it, he hears them, Maiko and Jason. It strikes him in the gut every time: what should be his.

Then why does he listen in?
What should be *his*. Entitlements.
The name Illtyd means *multitude of land*.

Jason once thrust … right into him. It brought water to his eyes.
The weight of him on top of him is the weight on top of him still.
Bulk.
Burden.

A new start?
A flee from that past and the stench of it?

He made a pit, and digged it, and is fallen into the ditch which he made.

30

The house says: *have I need of mad men, that ye have brought this fellow to play the mad man in my presence? Shall this fellow come into my house?*

The house knows all the books that were ever written. All the cultures. All the types. All those kinds of men and women: there really is no such variance. They are either bad or they are good. And one kind always tips the scales, one kind always prevails. That's usually how such stories go. The books have been written. This one not yet.

31

The toolshed.

No sooner has Jason entered (hesitatingly) than he has tripped on some rake or hoe and is sent crashing to the floor.

"You OK?"

The voice startles Jason, causing him to shriek like a little girl. Cut down to size again, this place, it does not suit him – a dead father calls across miles on winds to guilt him out; should never have left, and not even a wife to show for all his years here … and he's in a dirty toolshed and on such a dirty fucking night.

"It's me, Genki."

Jason breathes deeply, the situation needs a handle, and the smell from the man and the damp and the old rusty implements unused, functionless, and his father in the thrumfill of his ears gets only louder. A handle on it. Yes, he remembers now, the hobo on the dusty road, of course it was Genki, of course it was, they had even joked about the resemblance, and he recalls Pete panicking, crouching, hiding – it all makes complete sense now, unlike the night that was in the offing.

"You frightened the shit out of me!"

"Angel told you everything?"

Genki sometimes calls her that, even in English, he'll call her anything sweet to get that flash of teeth.

"Yes, Maiko told me everything. Or most of it."

The ridiculousness of it all still shakes him, how could it not? This is not what he had signed up for. And he is too hot-dog-Hollywood-American to not know what happens to pretty girls on rainy nights, and to the dumb musclemen who venture first.

But Pete? It's just that … well, what the hell *is* Pete? And how do you summon the strength to move a couch outside all by yourself?

"We're going to get out. Tonight, when he sleeps."

Genki, for all his faults, for all his filth, is a man with a plan. He's got to be: anything is an improvement on the way he currently stands, in blatant decrepitude, blatant desperation.

"And don't eat … the green stuff."

"Yeah, I know."

"Does he know you're out here?"

"He sent me out to check. Thinks it might be a wild animal that snuck in here."

"It is."

Genki's sadness prevents him from laughing at his own lame joke. Only Pete would find any of this remotely humorous.

"Did you bring me any food?"

Jason shakes his head. Guilt again. He hadn't even thought about it.

"Please throw something out soon. Anything. I'm fucking starving."

Genki knows to use *fucking* around the American. Natural English. Perfect inflection. It's something the tall man can relate to. Even in this gloom, looking him up and down with dark-adjusting eyes, Jason cannot quite reconcile Genki's vagabond appearance with the man he has always known. So far now is he from the affluent splendour of Roppongi Hills. So far from plush apartments, from expensive furniture, from fine wines he pretends to know about, deals going down with shrugs and nudges and winks – a man in control of a particular environment, professional, well off, married to a foreign woman you'd easily mistake for a fashion model, and unruffled, unmarred by a Tokyo that could be brutal were you not covered in some kind of invisible chainmail, a city can leave scars.

Here: stench, destitution, hunger … but a mounting mania for flight, if not revenge, no, no, not even that, just the getting out is all.

Home: the most beautiful word in any language.

To safety then.

And O! O! For a full stomach again.

Jason puts his spin on things:

"We leave him here. We'll just get out and leave him here. Put an end to it all. Call the police … I don't know."

"He's just got to be stopped, Jay. Just that, stopped."

When Genki says his name it's softer. More welcome. Tender. *Jay.* He cannot bear for Pete to say it ever again, it always comes out like a curse. He even sang a creepy song and freaked him out – why couldn't Pete just let the past be the past and move the fuck on?

He'll take that bloody knife himself, Jason will, and … well, he'll bloody do it, if given half a chance again … Jason steps closer to the filthy man and hugs him, despite the reek.

But the hugs have to hurry – Pete will be getting suspicious. He allows Genki the final words:

"A man who's lost everything he cares about, Jay … he's not going to think twice about doing any of us any harm. You know that, don't you? I've the sneaking suspicion he's done it before."

They said the pancreas was the worst place to get it. Not the doctors. The doctors didn't say that – they had more bedside manners than that, give them some credit – but he saw it on the Internet. The initial search had been a simple, even simple-minded one: cancer.

If you had it in the prostate it was easy enough to detect, and were you to catch it early, it could be treated – he'd have to get his own checked, and his Montana buddies could joke all the fuck they liked about being fingered in the ass and their childish fag jokes. But pancreatic cancer was no laughing matter. The symptoms were there right from the get-go. The darkened piss. The lighter-coloured shit. What an odd reversal that was. The loss of appetite: his grizzly father fading fast, tired all the time, not an ounce of energy. High temperatures. Hot one moment, then shivering as if an arctic wind was on him the very next. His own fault? Lifestyle? Perhaps. The lack of exercise, the bad diet, the packs of Camels didn't help, and the quarts of whiskey he tried to hide in the trunk of the car, ferrying the empties to the recycling centre.

He saw his father on his final deathbed, face wizened, more skeleton than anything else, a mere collection of bones, and two eyes that no longer held any light; the skin was stretched across the skull and it was yellow, no, a colour more like mustard.

His father moaned.

And the whole family moaned along with him, and Jason most of all, but not until that moment when they lowered him into the open ground; Jason remembered feeling a sense of relief knowing that the worms couldn't get to gnaw him all that much, the flesh of the big man had already been reduced to scant, from grizzly bear to grimly bare; there was nothing left but the bones, bare bones, and Jason felt relief that nothing now could gnaw his dad.

<h1 style="text-align:center">32</h1>

Maiko has a towel and is standing over a seated Jason, drying his wet hair. The rain had fallen coldly from the sky but now the wetness is hot and sticky in his tangled head-bush, the fair strands turned dark: it could be a metaphor for the situation in which they are so miserably ensconced.

They are whispering their conversation, everything delivered conspiratorially, low tones, watching over their shoulders, afraid that at any moment Pete could sidle up behind them, or not sidle, creep, just *creep* up behind them. The fucking creep.

Clashes and bangs and cutlery tings from the kitchen, so they're safe enough for the moment: Pete is still busy cooking: water boils, and something sizzles in a pan. He still has music playing, not so loud that it would impede him from tuning into other frequencies — the frequencies of his bandmates and what they might be up to.

LCD Soundsystem is the choice and an album that Pete likes, or not even *album*, but *record*, a word pretentious Pete insists on, throwback — his uncle would have stuck a needle in grooves, along with his hippy friends — as if using such words ordained on him some kind of authenticity, certainly a hold over the younger Japanese female; everything within the band, everything within the house was now a power struggle. The song that currently plays is called "I can change", but does Pete consider that proposal? Or is he focused on the cooking, the preparing? He places the green slices of gooseberry stems at the side of one of the plates.

"Genki was out there, right? In the toolshed?"

"We need to get him some food. Poor fucker. He's famished. Looks a state."

"We'll get him something. We'll find a moment."

"This whole thing, Maiko. It's fucking insane. I never knew Pete was so ... "

"So *what*? He has his reasons. They might not make sense to us ... but they do to him."

It's been taken from him.

His lover.

His music.

His sense of purpose.

Maiko throws the towel aside and takes Jason's face in her hands. She kisses him with urgent intent, tries to say so much in it, things she has no words for.

They are in this together.

She is looking into his eyes and thinking: I will never marry you, it doesn't work like that, but I will get us out of here. We *will* get out of this.

Is the foreigner getting all that in her eyes, in the exigency of the kiss?

"When this is all over, we start again. Just me and you this time."

Jason nods. He lets her continue. He reads nothing in her eyes. A kiss is just a kiss; women have always felt a need to be near him; things need to be spelled out.

"Genki will take care of us. But *we* must take care of him first. We've got to keep our ... "

Jason gives her time but she cannot complete the phrase. *Wits about us.*

"I know. I get that."

Would marriage be the completing of each other's sentences? She'd seen that in his American movies. And the resultant laughter, and the tripping over each other with things they so wanted to gush to each other, those celluloid couples, hardly enough space in time to get their sentiments out, so full of rush and affection and rush and desire, and the days were never quite long enough, so much more they wanted to squeeze in, those movie darlings, their meet-cutes, their hand-holding, getting it all out, terrific rushes, all out, and they stumbling in their gushings: *oh no, you first, no, no, you.* Her own father and mother never spoke much to each other. There were never any sentences to complete. Silence reigned over dinner tables. A harsh bulb hung – was it shadeless, or is that a self-pitying embellishment? The family: sitting there, each one enjoying each mouthful of food. Everything before them was delicious. There was effort put into that for sure. But not the conversation. Silence endured. Hours seemed to stretch. Someone told her that the philosopher, Schopenhauer – it must have been Pete, of course it was Pete – said that life was to be *endured* and not *enjoyed. Endured* was a new word for her then. She filed it away: it would surely be useful. That was what it was like at the dour dinner table. Silence. Yawning hours. The lunch table. The breakfast table too, even in the early mornings, when a trace of optimism should rightly have been present and correct, a new human day upon them, and what would that entail, hope? But beaten before it ever got off the ground. Even the picnics that the schools forced families to take part in, under unremitting July sun, a wide blue groundsheet placed under them and their plastic boxes spread out, full of carefully prepared treats, as the children played on swings and frolicked in water fountains. But there wasn't a whole lot ever said. Her father and mother seemed to be *enduring* life, so little joy in any of their transactions, as if each day was simply another set of tasks to be carried out. Only that. Only those. Tasks. They had jobs. They had duties. Days were like application forms and the boxes needing to be ticked; seemed more a form of bureaucracy than anything else; life: administrative. Perhaps that's why she turned to art. At least with music the idea of passion was concomitant. Couldn't be denied. The ones with passion were the ones who succeeded, right? Drive. What was there to say to each other at those picnics? *How was your day?* Just let the sun shine and the children play. There was little more anyone could do but that. Let that happen. It sufficed. But Maiko felt it even then. No hatred, nothing like that, her folks didn't hate each other, they just seemed like they couldn't be bothered to love, it seemed like effort, too much, bridges too far, the providing of food and shelter and warmth should be enough for any child, surely?

Maiko takes Jason's handsome face in her hands and kisses him once more. She doesn't love him. She's perfectly sure of that. She never will. She's not sure if she would even know how to go about it. How does one go about learning something like that, if it hasn't come naturally to you? It's not like language. The learning of a language had at least some rules. And even if you did learn it, the rudiments, how then did you go about showing it? From theory to practice. There may be lectures on it somewhere. Perhaps somebody has mapped it all out. Graphs. Pie charts. Ten rules for loving: a YouTube tutorial. This is how a young woman of her generation thinks. Give me the data, let me download it. But no, no, no, already it seems too late for all that; she has grown old over the last few days. Her face has aged, she can sense it, stress on the skin; has it been from the heat and the dust and the humidity and the constant sweat, or the storm outside (storms inside now too, the vortices there, the nerves of the stomach), the changes in temperature, up, down, inside the house, outside the house – what is this place? – each thunder bang carving another crease on her brow, each lightning strike etching another unwanted wrinkle. Or the situation. Is it the situation, the being there, in the house with these people, and the walls closing in. Or the music? Creation? Bad creation? An amalgamation of all these things? Most probably. When she gets back to the city, she wonders if people will even recognise her. (The house says nothing in response to her thoughts, lets her figure it out for herself.)

"Ready?"

He nods. It's about all he's able to do now. Words more and more seeming inadequate, action will be needed instead, for sure. Action. They brace themselves. A shout from the kitchen.

"Come and get it!"

The preparations have stopped. Their leader has summoned them.

Pete turns off the CD, and, once more, as if they hadn't heard the first time: "Come and get it!"

They go.

They go and get it.

Could she even find Sayuri? Like, if she went ahead and tried. Like, if she searched for her on a social media website, just keyed in her name, on Instagram or X, could she find her then? Where is she now? *Who* is she now? She could've gotten married; her family name could have changed, she could be at a silent dinner table with a silent husband, too.

Sayuri *what*?

Sayuri *who*?

She can't even remember what her family name was, way back then. Probably no point. Probably no point in going to the trouble.

Back then.

The room.

The seeking out of new terrains.

The vibrations in the bedroom, Maiko remembers those: doesn't want to let them disappear.

As if the air had been electrically charged.

And soon entering private spaces, releasing private moans that weren't private anymore but … shared; yes, a sense of sharing everything, the room, the day, the play.

Only *play*?

Or something more?

No, a searching is more than play, much more, it is the beginning of *adventure.*

How could Maiko ever find her again?

Sayuri.

Sayuri *what?*

Sayuri *who?*

And … if she did … if she did find her, then what?

Say what to her?

Do what?

Do you remember me?

They have grown. Everyone has grown old, you cannot stop that, only good music does not age.

And what if that girl, that girl with the big head and the sloping shoulders and the awkward gait – all endearing now, misty memory – what if that girl, now woman, said: *Sorry, I'm afraid I don't remember you. Who … who are you again?*

My name is Maiko. I tend to moan a lot.

And was the excitement then only because it was the first time? Was that where the tingling lay? That anticipation leading to what … *exhilaration?* The first time. The thin-limbed girl duly moaned under the curious touch of Maiko's fingertips. She made such an effort, that girl, such an effort to please, and to be pleased, and her thick lips moue-d to be kissed.

It had not even been with a boy … that first time.

With Jason, the weight of him on top of her; there was no excitement, not like that one true moment with Sayuri; the first time being touched, the nervousness giving way to innocent ecstasy. Counting each mole on her face, *beauty spots*, she referred to them as that, and Maiko connecting them. Dot to dot. And then a picture emerged. The shape you were looking for all the while. A perfect partner for a perfect afternoon. It took for only one of them to break that fix and glance at the other to get them both started, not a word, not a single word was necessary; a gulp perhaps, a dry swallowing: that was the only sound in the tense bedroom, hardly interrupting. And soon they were off and fondling. Soon they were entering private spaces, releasing private moans.

She can never go back.

Sayuri *what?*

Sayuri *who?*

Sometimes it feels like that is all she wants. To go back. For one day even. Wouldn't that be enough? Or hover over like an angel – Genki calls her *Angel* (she likes that, if she could change her name to an English one, that would be the one she'd choose). Hover over and observe. See the two young girls and their closeness and their tenderness. The world was so un-tender now. That's probably not even a word. *Un-tender:* Maiko tries to think what the English might be for the opposite of *tender*. If it's not *un-tender*, what is it? Probably just *rough*. The opposite of *tender* is probably only the word *rough*. Makes sense. That's the way life comes at her now. For everyone. Everywhere. Argue against that.

For a day.

Even for an hour.

Just hovering over.

Look at those two lovely girls. Before the world had taken hold on them. Re-live. She would kiss that girl, Sayuri, if the chance were given again. And she would perhaps not even go towards the girl's private parts, no, not even a gentle rub of those small nubs with their too-large nipples. No, she would just focus on her mouth. The mouth of the willing girl. Her full lips. And tenderly. Not rough, the way the storm-full world was now. Tenderly would be all.

33

A last supper.

It passed through Jason's mind.

His father had been a devout churchgoer, his big frame taking up most of the back pew in the little white church at the edge of town, his thin, po-faced wife beside him. Jason might not know the Bible as well as his bandmate – and Maiko knows not a word of it – but Jason knows enough to remember the famous last supper of Christ, and it passes his mind as they break bread here.

Pete doesn't make them say grace. In fact, since his cooking, he has been mild and relatively normal; there have been no thousand-yard stares, no glazing over, no eyebrow-raising and looks of mania in the eyes, not since the knife to Jason's temple.

Is Pete so quick to change or is Jason so quick to forgive and forget?

Perhaps he is the most Christian one after all – there's an irony in all this somewhere, if he were given time to reflect. Not much time for any of that. Still a quivering in his stomach – he sees the greens on the side of Maiko's plate. Only hers. Pete has marked his quarry. There are none on Jason's, none on Pete's own. How is Pete going to explain this one? Is it a taunt? A dare? Why doesn't Jason go ahead and ask him – he'll have a reason for it, an answer for everything. Steady, now. Be careful not to ruffle him. Jason knows they need to be strategic, in their moves, in their questioning.

Maiko remembers Genki's words, the ones she relayed back to her lover: *Whatever mad game all this is, we have to play along. We must make sure he thinks that all is going according to his plan.*

The three of them look rigid and uncomfortable, not for the first time since they've arrived in this peculiar house. They don't have instruments in their hands, appearing as if naked to each other: bare without hum or strum or beat. At least with a guitar in hand, or a drumstick in your fist, you can concentrate on that, can let it be your distraction. Nothing for them here though. Each other. A table. Seated. Stuck. Cutlery is all. The house itself seems to be groaning: must be the wind shaking it, nature letting known that it always surrounds and cannot be predicted, not to mind being tamed, the storm picks up again; they just hope the lights will stay on: American Jason can only take so many tropes, it would be just the thing for the lights to go out on them now and for the madman to be holding the knife and … but that's just imagination. They are a creative bunch. That's why they're here, to lay down tracks for a new album. *Lay down. Tracks.* Every word and phrase seem loaded when you are a learner and struggling with meaning and connotations. *Record.* The whole thing is probably all a grave misunderstanding. And if it isn't, well … they have the keys and all they have to do is make it to the van and get the hell on out of there. Simple really, isn't it? Simple as that.

Greens on the side of her plate. Hers only.

An electric fan is blowing, though with the cooler temperature now there is hardly any need for it; the blades revolve languorously, it's at the slowest speed, dispersing the cooking smells, clearing the air.

"Where'd you find that fan?"

"If you had looked properly, Jay, you would have noticed there were a few in boxes in the storage room. Just needed dusting off."

"Like our music, eh? Just needed a bit of dusting off."

It has only been a matter of hours since they played together in the white room, but already, in their minds, they are split up as a band, far apart as a unit. Already Maiko and Jason are in Tokyo doing different things, sipping cocktails in Genki's apartment and telling Melissa everything that had happened, and could she get her head around it, could she believe it, and had she any idea of what kind of person they were dealing with, and maybe talking to a journalist too, someone should be writing up this whole story … but who would believe a word of it?

Only thin green slices of stems on Maiko's plate.

"I don't know why you're looking so nervous, both of you. I have cooked before, you know."

Jason has picked up Maiko's lyrics notebook from a vacant chair and is leafing through it. He needs to focus on something other than the other faces at the table, focus on something other than what's on his lover's plate.

"You said earlier you were starving, mate!"

"Yeah … I don't know … just tired is all."

Maiko has enough tact to aim for cheeriness:

"The afternoon session went well. That's all that matters. You were right to get us out in the air for a while. Nature. All that."

The three raise their beer cans and bump them together.

They are split up as a band, far apart as a unit, but only two of them seem aware of this fact at this particular moment.

"Well, what are you waiting for? Dig in."

34

The house says: no, do not dig *in*. Dig *out*. Dig *outside*. See what you'll find there.

Is everything buried around here?
Deep.
Deep wells.
Is the house referring to the land or the people?

Some things do not remain buried, some things want to crawl back out from where they've been stuffed, like zombies back onto the turf to confront the living, the wrongdoers. Has the house said all this before?

The house finds that it is repeating itself, but no harm in that, because history does, because people keep on doing the same things, the same mistakes.

The house sighs. The people inside the house will think it is just the wind, the tempest rising.

No, do not dig *in*. Dig *out*. Dig *outside*. See what you'll find there.

35

Apprehensively, knives cut and forks are taken to open mouths; they feed themselves, these creatures, no different are they from any other, needing: food, shelter, mates.

Pete watches the couple, and their smiles try to convey the notion that they are happy to be in this house with them, even though the winds hammer harsh again and the house seems to shake in its wake.

"Well?"

"Delicious. Didn't know you had it in you."

Pete didn't bother laying out chopsticks, wants to see the blades of knives, see tines, see sharp things that can penetrate, poke – and look at Maiko's teeth, how white they are! How has she managed to be unstained by coffee or tea or beer? And her face so plainly beautiful, beautifully plain, when she pulls the hair away from it and allows its reveal. There are so many old folk songs about killing lovers, killing beautiful women, the bludgeoning of beautiful wives. Those are great old songs: Pete wishes he could remember some of them. He's heard them for sure, countless times: the old hippy friends of his uncle would have known them for sure, chirruping them out on old Spanish guitars in dubious tunings: "Down by the Willow Garden" ... that was one, wasn't it? It rings some bell for him. And Nick Cave had recorded a whole album of them, *Murder Ballads*, ha, he remembers that, the mid-90s, and the lanky, morose Australian whacking Kylie Minogue over the head down by the water. *All beauty must die.* And Jason too, his, *his* Jason, so handsome here – the setting isn't exactly romantic, but Pete has done his best for them; they should have candles really, a romantic candle in the centre of the table, how nice that would have been, that idea never occurred to him. Romance. He never really thinks of that at all. Well, he can't think of everything. Those hippy girls and their tie-dye shirts and their stink of flowers and weird oils and Uncle letting them stay for weeks on end and they never had any money and they would even stay in his bedroom and often even in his own bed, cuddling up to him, and how was he supposed to sleep with the smell of them, and they didn't even shave their legs like attractive women should. No wonder he still has trouble sleeping. No wonder he can be up all night, pottering about, looking for, looking for something…

He keeps his eyes on their movements.

Jason has to keep the game going, too. Conversation. He must keep in mind Genki's advice: *Whatever mad game all this is, we have to play along.*

"Where did you learn?"

"Learn what?"

"To cook?"

"Oh, my uncle, he loved the kitchen. Showed me a few tricks. And I picked up a few more things when I came to Japan."

Maiko impales a *maitake* mushroom on her fork and holds it up.

"Like these. You're a fungi expert, aren't you?"

Pete shrugs. He notices that she has not touched any of the greens on the side of her plate. When will she try them? When? And will she question as to why Jason and Pete have none on their plates? Is she that stupid? Is she as dumb as he thinks she is? All women, that stupid, can't even notice things. The stink of them and their hair and their heads on his own pillow as he tried to sleep as a boy – what chance? It was probably true, now that he thinks of it, that his mother threw herself in, it was probably true, just threw herself away, the way she did, abandoned life, what was worth sticking around for? Bible and booze? The mad malevolence of males? Bottom of Mywngil. The lake bed. She might be there still. Picked at by pike. Eels slipping in and out of the spaces between her ribs. They said all kinds of terrible things about her. They said all manner of things about his father too, downright horrible the things they cried out, shouted at him as he made his way through wet Welsh streets: *Crazy cunts! Whole lot of 'em should be locked up!* And his uncle too, they said things about him: *Smelly old, washed-up beatnik, that time was gone,* said things, so many things, said things, cried out, shouted at him, *locked up and the key thrown away,* how was he to make his way to school even, *and good riddance,* an ordinary day, cold winds, threadbare jumper, bullies set to pounce, shouted about each and every one of his clan. Clan! Where did that come from? *Clan!* Just popped in. He prefers *band. Band* suggests … They are always forced to think about language because Maiko is always around and because of the country they have found themselves in. There's always some kind of translation going on, things moving from one language to another. Sometimes it's unclear. Sometimes things get lost along the way, or mangled. If it was just Jason and himself, if it was just the two of them, things would be a whole lot clearer. No barriers. Clear communication. And maybe they should just get out, maybe the two of them should just get out of the country altogether, start again, a fresh start, yes. New band. Band of brothers. Somewhere else. Somewhere completely different. Laos. Brazil. Mexico. He's done it before. Got out. Got away. Anywhere would be fine. Venezuela. Cambodia. New York fucking City. There would be no need for anyone to translate then, no need to explain things to the dumb bitch; they'd know each other's tongues, just the two of them. Tongues. Their tongues could once again wrap around each other. He has always wanted a band, to be in a band, to be the leader of a band. It didn't have to be four or five people. It didn't have to be the rhythm section of bass, drums, didn't have to be the front two of guitar and vocals, they didn't have to go the whole hog, didn't have to be like all the others … just two. Two would be enough. Duo. Two would be sufficient if they were close and got on well and understood each other and didn't even have to think at all really, just knew each other so well that one would know what the other was trying to do or was going to play … like telepathy. That sense of connection. He always wanted that. That closeness. They stank out the bloody bedroom! Could even smell it coming from out between their legs, filth … and all he wanted was to get some sleep and go to school the next day and not get the shit kicked out of him on the way. Jason had thrust himself into him. Jason had leaned on Pete in the classic Bowie-leaning-on-Ronson pose. *You know your 70s rock. I'm a guitarist. Welcome to the club.* Band suggested … band suggested …

"Jason" was a song by Perfume Genius and it often rolls around inside Pete's head, because Pete thinks a lot about Jason, thinks of little else, and when it was just the two of them, and when it was just the two of them, band, bond … and how much *easier* it was. Isn't that what everyone wants out of life? No complications. Ease. A normal mum and dad, and if there was to be an uncle, let it be someone who is not so *alternative,* but the kind of man who just slipped him a few quid for the arcade games … but the people that invaded his space.

Easier.

How they could just … focus on one another.

Pete and Jason.

Jason and Pete.

He was under the impression then that nothing could come between them. Nothing.

And then, Genki suggested a female singer. Someone alluring. Someone that would be "front and centre". Sex appeal. Look at her! She's got something. It was enough, enough for Jason to fall.

And Jason fell.

The American is looking at the lyrics notebook again.

"You now when you asked about words to describe our sound … I'm sorry I was being such a dick. You were right. I thought about it. And I think words like, *wild*, and *altitude*, and *copse*, because we're like, like, close to one, like … makes me feel … that's what we should be making."

"That's good, Jay. I'm glad you saw sense. Glad you put some thought into it."

"They could even be titles. With Maiko singing over the ambient sounds … like a Cocteau Twins track … like 'Fotzepolitic' … minus the twangy guitars of course."

"Wait. Wait," she says. "I'm lost. Slow down. First, I don't know what a *copse* is. I thought that was a dead body."

"No, no, that's *corpse*. A dead body. A *copse* just means … like … woods … like a small forest."

Pete looks at Jason. No one is eating now. Their faces fixed on each other. Maiko needs to know more.

"And you said *twins?*"

"Cocteau Twins. A band. Before your time. Before our time too, really, but the singer had a great voice, like yours."

Pete stays sullen. He sees Maiko pushing around the pieces of food on her plate, the thin green slices are still there, untouched.

"You should eat your greens, Maiko. Hasn't your mother ever told you that before? I was sure that Japanese mothers pushed all kinds of vegetables on their little darlings. Healthy, like, you know."

She looks down at her plate. Eventually … she may have to.

Jason fidgets with the lyrics notebook, with his glass of beer, with his knife and fork as they rattle too loudly on the plate: antsy, uneasy, does she have to; does she really have to put them in her mouth?

Knife edge.

She cuts a piece of gooseberry stalk and forks it into her mouth.

Pete smiles, "Very nutritious. It will be great for your voice. Just you wait and see. You'll sing like … *an angel.*"

Maiko takes her can of beer to her lips and when Pete drops his eyes to his own plate for the briefest of seconds, she spits the chewed green goo into the mouth of the can. Timing. Crucial. He doesn't catch any of it. He takes a swig from his own beer and stares at her:

"Well? How does it taste?"

"Bit bitter. But fine."

She pictures it falling to the bed of the beer can. Sludge. Poisoning the drink. A corruption.

"How come I don't get any?"

"It's for her voice. You won't be singing."

Maiko pretends that she's just realized something:

"Shit. I forgot to put more beer in the fridge, no cold ones."

She looks at Jason, "Can you go get some?"

Now it's his turn to pretend, to perform, and he starts to write something in the notebook, as if distracted by a sudden and incontrollable burst of creativity.

Pete sighs and rises.

"Right, I'll go."

"Oh, you're such a gentleman. See that, Jason, a typical British gentleman. You could learn a thing or two."

Her thoughts are contrary to everything she says – her thoughts are back with the slap in the woods: hard hand across her face; yes, he had smacked her bloody hard, and she had fallen to the forest floor and sobbed, shocked and sore – it would be a long time before that scene ever fades from her.

While Pete makes his way to the side storeroom, Jason springs into action. Quickly he tears a page out of the notebook and takes the rest of the green slices off Maiko's plate. He folds the greens up in the paper, runs to the dustbin and flings it all in. Maiko hands him her beer can and he empties it down the sink, then adds the empty can to the gunge of the trash receptacle. The whole series of movements is carried out so rapidly that Jason's heart pounds to its intensity. This is what he has been reduced to: he now fears the man he has known for years; fears the man he'd thought a friend.

How has it all come to this? He could beat the fucking crap out of the guy if he wanted. If he put his mind to it. Look at their sizes. Compare physiques: the tall and muscular, the squat and portly. And yet he does not even consider entering that arena. Why not? Is he under some kind of spell, trapped, playing the game Genki had told him to play – or is it just that Pete actually *is* the more powerful of the two, the most powerful of them all?

And what does that mean – *power*? Where does it come from? And what kind of strength would you need to pull that heavy couch outside; does some kind of delirium take hold?

When Pete returns with the beer from the storeroom refrigerator, he sees them studiously studying the lyrics notebook. So much pretence, the game, the game…

He asks them if there are any lyrics worth reading aloud to him. They shrug. No one on the same page.

They continue to distractedly eat until there is nothing left on their plates. The band leader is impressed.

"Well done you two. Your parents would be proud."

There is a hint of suspicion in his eyes, but the game continues, their fakery.

"No, well done *you*. That was delicious," says Jason.

Maiko stands. "Let me clear up," she says.

They get up from the table and leave the kitchen while the woman brings the plates to the sink. She stares out the window hoping to catch Genki's attention.

Is he watching?

Is he out there in the clamour?

Is he there?

She waves.

She is watching TV with her family and an old American drama is playing.

In one particular scene the father of the family comes home from a hard day at the office and puts his briefcase down in the hallway of the glamorous home.

An aproned, flour-smeared wife comes out of the busy kitchen to greet him and welcome him, and she plants a kiss on his stubbly-but-handsome cheek, until he surprises her by grabbing her by the waist and pulling her petite frame towards him and kissing her passionately.

This is what goes on?

This, the everyday?

Maiko's father moans.

The kiss is suspended and the man tosses his hat, nonchalantly. Expertly it lands on the hook on the wall. He loosens his business tie, letting air in at his neck, and the wife watches him, all his graceful, masculine movements, her 1950s eyes a-twinkle, as if she's been waiting for him all day long, and how dull it was without him, this man of her dreams.

Young Maiko is thinking how wonderful if this actually *is* the everyday, if it *could be*, if this is what actually goes on in the houses of other lands. Does it? Does it go on in other lands? It certainly does not go on here.

Her father rises from his armchair and stomps his way out of the living room and up the stairs, letting it be known exactly what he thinks of all this nonsense, without offering a single word. It is a lesson for his daughter. He is telling her that there is a difference between fantasy and reality. And that she must learn this for herself.

His bedroom door shuts. He has to go to work the following day. Naturally.

Maiko's mother hasn't made a single sound during the whole episode, the TV episode, or her husband's. She has not moaned. She has kept her eyes on the big-backed Hitachi TV. Maiko cannot fathom as to her mother's thinking.

Does it go on?

Does it?

In other lands?

Passionate kisses and words of endearment.

And why doesn't it go on here?

No answers are forthcoming.

She'll learn for herself.

Soon her mother rises and heads up the same stairs – it's less of a stomp, more of a weary trudge. She has to go to work the following day, too.

36

Hunkered down, but Genki rises when he sees her wave from the kitchen. His angel. Perhaps if he had not married Melissa, he would have married her. There was something about her, some inner pain he wanted to alleviate, something inside of her that was trying to squirm out – he is thinking of art of course, not anything physical, some form of expression, music most probably. Maiko is often lost in her thoughts, softly moaning to herself when she thinks no one can hear her, but Genki hears, and he wonders about her. Perhaps she is pondering her past, something he knows nothing about, or perhaps she is contemplating her future, which is something he can do something about.

He waves back.

The whole situation is crazy … but crazy situations happen. This land is full of them. You can be going about your business on an ordinary day when suddenly the whole place can shake and buildings topple right in front of you. Just like that. It doesn't seem to make sense, until you study the science and realise there are huge plates underneath your feet and they have a tendency to move. It isn't the pantheistic Shinto gods of old Japan. It is nothing to stir the superstitious or the silly; it is plain and ordinary science; the plates of the planet, they move, and if you are in the wrong place at the wrong time … then that is that. *Curtains*, Melissa said, and that had to be explained to him, and he uses that expression himself now: that if they didn't get a few decent tracks down it was *curtains* for them, and he'd have to move on to other acts that would hold more promise. The business is cutthroat, you have pretty much one shot; all the arts are like this, your elevator pitch has to be sharp and prepared, no one has time to listen to any other old bullshit these days. Sharp. Be prepared. When you meet the man or woman in the expensive suit with your pitch, you have roughly ten seconds of sample sounds to make your case, maybe thirty seconds of your finest practised palaver. That is the extent of it. If the man or woman (in a better suit than yours) is not impressed, well, you have to tell your charges to go back to the practice warehouse or to that boxy apartment and continue with their own miserable-music-making with Pro Tools or whatever software that has sucked them in in the first place.

No time now though.

No time now to be pondering the industry.

Night is upon them, and darkness, in more ways than one, is upon them, and they have to figure out a way out of all this.

But Maiko's wave from the kitchen is a promising start.

Food at least, at last; she'll have a few scraps for him.

She turns to make sure no one is behind her, and when the coast is clear she leans over the sink, pulls across the stiff kitchen window and starts to drop bananas, vegetables in foil wrapping, and a bottle of water out the window: they plop to the mud below and she hopes that he will be the first animal to get to them. Every living thing is hungry out there. You have to be fast and you have to have your wits about you. She can't see clearly what is happening – the darkness, the clamorous weather – but she has faith in the manager who has never given up on her, and who'd surely not give up on himself.

Fast like a dog on all fours, Genki is out of the toolshed and grabbing the food. He stuffs it into his ragged shirt and torn pockets. Back to the toolshed he runs, low, crouched – this is what he has been reduced to: someday he might look back and laugh at the farcicality of it all, but not now, definitely not now. Now he has got nothing at all to laugh about.

Maiko sees a reflection in the window behind her as she closes it. She gasps with fright.

"Oh my God! You scared me!"

Pete is standing at the kitchen door, watching her.

She cannot tell whether the contorted creases around his mouth are in ironic sneer, or the beginnings of a reprimanding scowl.

"What are you doing?"

He doesn't give her a chance to respond; his next question is louder:

"Why is the kitchen window open?"

"Just…actually I'm feeling a little dizzy. Just wanted to let in some fresh air." She clutches her stomach. "Period pains."

Surely that is enough. Surely he won't ask her to actually *prove* it.

The subject seems to throw him.

He looks away from her and says, more softly this time, "Right, you should maybe go to bed and rest. Maybe you ate too much."

He thinks she has eaten the green slices of gooseberry stems. He thinks she is poisoned and will expire during the night. He has gotten it all wrong, and that is all right with Maiko: it feels like some kind of result…but she will not rest on it.

She makes a show of closing the window, as if the reaching for it is an inordinate struggle. She tries to keep her hands from shaking…steady now, play his game, do not let him know that anything is amiss.

When she turns around, he is right there in front of her, close now, way too close, invading her personal space and sniffing at her like a wolf.

She tries to remain composed, but it is not easy: his nose nearly meets hers.

He puts out his hand and touches her belly, softly, revolving, revolving, his palm is on her and doing slow revolutions, like a black 45 spinning on a record player.

"Here. Is here where it hurts?"

Like he cares. Like he gives a shit.

"Yes."

"When plants that are not native, start to encroach on other native plants of an area … they call that … *invasive*. Some plants are *invasive*."

The botanist.

He keeps circling his hand round her lower abdomen, circling circling, and his words seem to have the same effect, revolving around her ears, they are hypnotic.

She tries not to look into the whorls of his eyes but there is nowhere else to look. His breath smells as much of beer as her own. She feels they are both unclean, dirty creatures. She feels foul.

The heat of the kitchen brings a droplet of sweat to her brow. The night is getting close and clammy again.

"Some plants just want it all. To be front and centre. Not caring about what goes on behind. Just wanting the light. The light. Just wanting the light to grow, to grow tall, even if really they are very small. Do you see what I mean?"

She is nodding. She sees what he means. Though why she did not see all this months ago?

He takes his hand away; he sniffs at it. He smiles at her.

"Some dogs can sniff cancer in people. Did you know that? They are so finely attuned to the human body, their noses so sensitive, their senses so fine, they can actually sniff out disease in frail folk. Remarkable, isn't it?"

She nods. It is all she can do now. Is she even breathing? She must be because she can smell him. They both stink. They both need showers again. This place, the filth of the house and the situation and the weather and the countryside, the whole lot of it – she moans internally, wanting out, wanting out, wanting out of everything.

He steps back from her and becomes an entirely other person. He is smiling now, the kind of smile he gives when an hour of music rehearsal has gone well, or when he's hit the right note at the right time, or when Jason is near him and they are in complete accordance.

"Yes. Rest. An early night. I'm sure you'll feel right as rain in the morning."

Maiko is still nodding. There are tears in her eyes. The more of them that trickle down her face, the more he smiles at her.

"Strange expression, isn't it? *Right as rain.* There's one for your notebook. Maybe even a song title. You can learn so much from me. But like I said, teachers can be dangerous. My uncle was a teacher by profession, you know. But he gave it all up to pursue a more alternative lifestyle. A different kind of dangerous."

He steps to the window and gazes out.

"English, the language, plants, relationships … so much to learn."

Maiko's tears continue to trickle down.

Suddenly a shout from the music room: Jason is a man desirous, and clueless as to what is happening: "I'll take another beer!"

"Your boyfriend is calling you. *Your* boyfriend. Not *mine.* Why don't you be the good little subservient Japanese girl and bow before him and serve your master. That's what you do, isn't it?"

She tries to leave but he blocks her path.

"Just remember whose band it is, right? For however long you have left."

He laughs then as he lets her pass.

She leaves him standing alone in the kitchen, looking out the window.

A king can, he thinks for a moment, but it's dark outside, and there's only his own reflection looking back at him, and it's not a sneer at the corner of his mouth, it's a scowl, his whole face is nothing but a scowl.

Genki? Are you still out there? I should have finished you when I had the chance. *For we all stumble in many ways. And if anyone does not stumble in what he says, he is a perfect man, able also to bridle his whole body.* I won't make those kinds of mistakes again.

37

The house says: washed, washed in this rain, but not feeling cleansed.

Too much squalor reigns within, too much coarseness and pollution, too many problems, no solutions.

No harmony here: walls can feel it and floors are sick with the stomps of their feet.

The house says: if you do not take your fucking poisons elsewhere... you will leave the house no option.

38

Pete saunters into the white music room and hands Jason the beer he requested.

"Cheers."

He has been listening back to the efforts of earlier and the tracks coming out of the speakers now sound pretty good to him: they have made him relaxed, serene; it is as if he has forgotten about everything else.

"Some good stuff here, seriously. Tomorrow could even be better."

"Could be a rough night though."

"Why?"

"Your girlfriend says she's not feeling well. Maybe the food didn't agree with her. I'm awfully sorry… my cooking."

"Maybe I should go and check on her."

"Maybe you should."

As Jason is about to rise from his seat, Pete puts a gentle hand on his shoulder. What's this a play for? Tenderness? Compromise? But still… sorrow in his eyes.

"You could stay down here a little longer. Let her sleep. I've put a fan in your room. It'll cool her. Why don't you stay and… "

"No, Pete. No. For fuck's sake!"

From sorrow to bitterness, all hurt hurtling so fast…

"You should do what I fucking say."

"Stop with all this weird shit. You're not in control of us. You're not in control of anything."

Jason rises tall.

His teeth are grinding into each other and his fists are clenched, sending ripples and twitchings along his meaty arms; he was told to play the game and he is in danger of losing it now. He could take the cunt out, right here and now, just lay him out. But it's not part of the plan. He has to think of Maiko, and Genki.

"Shit. You can hit me if you want. I don't mind. Jay, what's more pain?"

"I'm not going to hit you, Pete. Just … let's just call it a day."

"I liked it when you were rough."

Jason shakes his head; he puts the beer on the coffee table as gently as he can (he wants to smash it against the wall) and leaves the room.

Pete remains.

He stands for a moment, listening to Jason making his way up the creaky stairs, listening in, always listening in, as if the sounds are there to direct him, guide him – maybe that's why music is the true salve, the only thing that can quiet an unquiet mind.

He waits.

When the house is quiet, he begins to remove his clothes, almost ceremoniously. The thoughts are coming now, the thoughts deliberate at first and soon like a fighter plane up in the sky and strafing – the quiet mind is never that quiet for very long.

He stands naked. He goes to a shelf in the corner of the room and from behind an old book he takes a white headband and ties it around his forehead. Haruki: this is how he wore it … Warrior. A warrior pose. *Look powerful, don't I?* Under the gooseberry bush. Wonderer. *Playing gooseberry,* he told her: *someone who gets in the way, especially in the way of love, in the way of passion.* Third wheel. The fucking dirty cunts were in his own bed and on his bedroom floor and once he opened the bathroom door and his uncle was in the shower with two lanky long-haired sluts and the dirt sliding off them and down the drain.

Pete closes his eyes and rubs his hands along his body. *It's no use just posing. No use assuming the stance. You have to commit.*

He shivers at his own touch; it is cooler now that night has fallen, the terrible heat of the day abated, and his eyes shut tight, making him look like he is in pain.

Perhaps he is.

Haruki.

The family home.

So many things buried.

He opens his eyes and looks around. What was that he had thought of earlier? A king can. Must retrieve that thought, retrieve that notion now, that self-building, that self needs re-building. Yes, a king can. Not just a pose. Be confident. Take what's yours. Take what's rightfully yours. *When thou liest down, thou shalt not be afraid: yea, thou shalt lie down, and thy sleep shall be sweet. Be not afraid of sudden fear, neither of the desolation of the wicked, when it cometh.*

Does she swim at the bottom of the lake and is the water brown down there? Are her eyes open and she sees it all quite clearly, sees Pete and his problems, his betrayers.

He leaves the room and doubts that music will ever be made there again. Not by three of them at least. Not that. One of them will have to go. She's already on the way out. *Third wheel*, ha! That should have been the name of the band. Cunts. Cunts, listen to me, I have a name for the band: Third Wheel, but get this, there'll only be two people in the band! Pete and Jason. Geddit? There will be no longer a third wheel, because it will be only two! Genius. The stairs do not creak when he walks up them, for he knows the volatile ones, he knows the ones to be avoided, the ones you do not tread on; he moves like a ghost.

On the futon, clothed, a fan blowing on them (he must have put it there for them, his preparedness), they hear footsteps near their door.

And just outside they spy the shadow of a body underneath the frame: guess who?

This is their cue.

Maiko pretends to start retching into the waste paper basket – it is convincing; she could've been one of those tawdry actresses in those cheap daytime dramas, she'd fool you for sure. She retches for all she's worth.

Naked, his ear pressed to the door, he is listening in on Maiko's moans, her puking. He is smiling, pleased with himself, this is all his doing. He has broken that third wheel. Soon Jason will be wretched and bowing before him, *yea, mine own familiar friend, in whom I trusted, which did eat of my bread,* and asking to be taken back and held and comforted and loved, *deliver my soul from the sword,* loved properly.

The play continues.

She retches and Jason makes consoling sounds, and it seems to be working a treat as the shadow disappears from outside the door; Pete making his naked way back to his own room, thinking his mission complete, and the American man holds the Japanese woman, and they will wait for the crazed one to sleep, and for the house to fall silent to the witching hours and then, then they will get ready to depart.

Before he retires to the futon Pete takes the photographs from the little drawer. He looks at them and smiles, holding them to his chest.

He pulls one cool sheet around his body, it'll be enough to keep him warm in a still warm room, a room that had morning sun and retained it.

This isle, he thinks, is full of noises, but quiet now. He is quiet now, this Caliban preparing for sleep; sometimes a thousand twangling instruments hum about his ears, even in sleep, sounds and sweet airs and sometimes voices, and if he wakes after long sleep, maybe the clouds will open and show riches.

But he never has *long sleep*. Usually short spurts, before he is up and prowling again, at it again – night cannot ever contain him.

For now though, his breath becomes regular, and the old photographs slip from his grip and slide down his side, as the night begins to win over, capturing him (but for how long, how long?). He will sleep, sure, give in, sure, but for how long, how long?

39

The house says: well, what do we have here? What now? And how will it turn out? Tantrum, tumult, torture? Is that the order?

He can't be really sleeping, surely, that one, what with the wind blowing hard and that shed door banging again.

Look at those shut eyes, little flickers, seems like they could spring open and alive at any moment; so much pretence with these people, the roles they play.

So, what now? What now?

... in the secret places he doth murder the innocent ...

The house awaits, bated breath.

40

Furtive movements, furtive as alley cats, or wilder yet, lynxes or leopards, careful not to make a sound – their backpacks are on their backs and they try not to make a single sound: soft they pad around, delicate footfalls to the floor.

One accidental creak on the stairs freezes them with momentary panic, but they'll wait it out, won't budge, and when the creak elicits no response from the closed room where the third man sleeps, they decide to carry on.

Does the third person really sleep?

Down the stairs they creep, hearts in mouths, and when they arrive at the bottom they can afford one sigh of relief. So far so good. Still no noise from Pete's room. The master's bedroom. The fucking master. Fucking monster. They will be so happy to get out and never see that man again. This is their plan.

Into the main room they silently go. Jason rushes to Pete's laptop and pulls a USB flash memory stick from the side of it, whispering: "A memento."

"He'll go nuts if he thinks he's lost that, too."

"Like he's not already over the edge. You want to push him a little more?"

Jason turns on the computer and shudders when it sounds its heraldic unnecessary notes. They grimace, but again, no sounds come from above, they must think themselves safe. He deletes all the files. He leaves the computer completely blank. He figures it's the least he can do: erase all the work they have done. Pete deserves that. Pete deserves a lot more, but they do not have the time, they need to just get out, flee, for fuck's sake, flee! He pockets the memory stick and in American whispers again: "Let's get the fuck outta here."

It has stopped raining but the wind still huffs hard.

So much changing, to and froing, warm winds to cold, sweat to shivers, how could anyone acclimatize to any of this?

Perhaps it is just this place; it had felt *off* to Jason the minute he set foot in the place. Some intuition, right from the get-go.

They set their course away from the house, crouching low, heading for the toolshed, its door still open and walloping – Jason had thought he had closed it, when he went out to see Genki ... they had closed it, hadn't they? But there it is, banging away, and if that wouldn't wake you – can Pete possibly sleep through that? Can he?

And then ...

And then ...

What they are about to witness ... it will never ever leave them.

It will moan in their nightmares for as long as they are to live, on their deathbeds even, perhaps even then, this sight will manifest before them, a sight that will assure them that they are better off leaving this diseased world, and how loving will be the concord and nothingness of death, away from the horror which inside this shed awaits.

Jason steps in and is the first to see it.

Right there in front of them ... is Genki's head, in a puddle of its own blood, and it is separated from Genki's body.

"Jesus Christ!"

When Maiko sees it, she lets loose such a cataclysmic howl, would put any other crazed and savage beast to shame.

The blood is everywhere. Even in the dark they can see it has sprayed and spattered around the decaying walls of the rotten place, on every tool, and the stench of it assaults their nostrils.

Maiko turns aside and throws up.

She didn't have to ingest any poison, Pete had some extra, far more potent poison prepared, and this was it. This image. The sick one has made her extremely sick. Violently so. Eternally so. It will continue to manifest, and manifest again, even at the very end. All this. All this sickness and violence and…

"He did this, didn't he? When?"

Jason is too dumbstruck to answer.

"How could anyone…? This isn't even…is this even happening?"

Genki's eyes are open.

The dead eyes of their music manager.

Staring at them.

Forever.

They have to get away from here, or the same will happen to them. Get anywhere, anywhere else, get anywhere, just get the fuck out.

Jason turns and pulls her by the hand. It is almost as if she's forgotten how her body works, how limbs are supposed to move, how a body walks or runs, strings cut like Sayuri's strings, a marionette falls, needs no puppet master, lifeless, collapsed…but adrenalin has kicked in for Jason and he pulls at her hand, dragging her from the old shed and shedding the diabolical sight and into a night which only increases in its wails of wind.

They run to the van and Jason fumbles for his keys. He drops them in the mud but is able to finally stop his trembling hand enough to open the damn door.

So many trembling hands, this place, as if the land is set forever on vibrate, constantly sending shocks through the soles of their feet and up and through them, their eyeballs could very well burst out on stalks like in a grotesque animation. His Scooby Doo jokes don't seem so funny now, this is the real thing, and the villain has already been unmasked.

For a moment they try to collect themselves.

Breathing heavily, they just sit there, staring vacantly out, watching the trees sway in the wind.

"It's OK, Maiko. There are no lights on in the house. He's sleeping. He'll never know we met."

"But when did he even do it? Maybe he didn't go to bed. He must have crept back out. He's always prowling around, you know that. Maybe he's not actually in bed now … where the fuck is he?"

He reaches over and holds her hand, looking her in the eye. "We're OK. I promise. We're going to get out of here. Just you and me now, it's just the two of us. OK?"

Jason sticks his key in the ignition, and just as the van sputters to life, the CD player automatically starts up too.

But it is not one of his legendary rock CDs.

It is not The Ramones.

It is not The Replacements, Pixies or Fugazi.

Instead, it's a recognizable voice that sends shivers down their spines.

"Thought you could leave, did you, Jay? Thought you could just drive away and leave me here."

The fuck!?

Pete starts humming, the same tune to the song "Jason".

"Can't remember all the lyrics now, but something about *knowing a lot* … that comes up, wasn't that it? And *love where there always should have been some*. Something like that anyway."

Laughter then.

Maniacal.

Hair-raising.

Maiko pushes the eject button and the CD slides silkily out.

On it, written in thick black magic marker: *No one ever truly leaves me*.

Jason rolls down the window and throws the disc into the nearby bushes.

Maiko yells at him. "Drive! Just fucking drive! We've got to get away! I can't take it!"

But there *is* more to take. He's not yet done with them, for when Jason puts his foot to the pedal, from behind them, emerging, a head, between them again, the band leader, the third wheel, the gooseberry, bitter, leaves a tart taste wherever he goes … and the band leader has the sword in his hand.

The couple shriek in unison and the van careens.

Jason tries to steer the vehicle but he struggles to keep it on path – Pete falls back and starts clambering to right himself, the tip of the sword nicking him on his banded forehead as he does so.

More blood for the endless evening, just more of it.

Maiko cannot put a dam to her banshee screams, they are feral, frantic, fearful, and she's trying to open the door of the van to let herself out.

All the while Pete's laughter grows only louder, a hyena stumbling upon fresh carrion – who knew it could all have turned out to be so much fun?

Jason stomps on the brake and they both tumble out from the front of the van and take to the thickets.

Copse, he had said.

And *woods.*

And *forest.*

So many names for what was just a collection of trees … and they are everywhere around now, tall and dark and imposing and each and every one an obstacle.

They find each other and they run together.

But where can they possibly go?

They gesture to each other, turn around; circling back, that's where they should be going, back to the van, where they need to be, but they are fleeing in the wrong direction.

Pete kicks the back doors open and jumps out of the vehicle. He is bare-chested, wearing jeans, and yes, that is a white headband tied around his forehead, the nick of blood making a red circle right at its centre.

Rustling through the bushes.

Things always on the move.

Things hardly ever settling.

Always foraging, running to or running from – it's the latter for the human couple scared out of their wits, and scampering almost blindly.

Pete follows, just as blind in the dark, laughing madly to himself, and to the night forest he spills his decree:

"You can't leave the band, Jay! We have music to make. Oh, Jaybird! We were meant to be together."

Sing-song. Sinister.

His eyes are squints in focus, trying to locate: where have they disappeared to… but their jostling through the undergrowth is enough for him to track, they are not far off at all, he'll be upon them in no time.

"*Hear diligently my speech, and my declaration with your ears. Behold now, I have ordered my cause.*"

He trots, a confidence about him now, sword in hand; no, they are not that far ahead.

"*I am like a pelican of the wilderness: I am like an owl of the desert. O Jaybird!*"

He swipes at brush and fern and bush, whatever stands in his way. He jogs, hitting at branches, scattering leaves, whatever impedes. He stops swinging the sword then, instead picking up his running pace; he must not lose them. Must not. Must not. Needs to put an end to the moaning bitch and her disciple, take back what is rightfully his:

Took his eyes off the digital device to look fully at the man with the American accent. This size of his eyes had expanded in surprise, overcome by the sheer physical delight. His hands developed a tremor, and he tried his best to conceal it.

You know your 70s rock. Welcome to the club.

If there had been music playing and he had been singing or playing along, things would have been different, calmer, but he had no such crutch. Nothing to lean on. Lean on Mick Ronson, like Bowie. Looks like we're up. The two arose and went to the performance area … and they sang together.

He told us not to blow it!
Together!
He knows it's all worthwhile!

41

The house breathes a sigh of relief. All three of them are out of it now. Would that it would stay that way … and they just … stay away: *These three have robb'd me.*

But the house still hears, for still they run, close enough … what chaos they cause with every turn.

A house and its gardens are supposed to be places of accord – they got it all wrong, these infidels of order, they have brought anything but harmony, a stain upon the terrain.

42

Pete Illtyd has his nose in the air and sniffs like a wolf. His nostrils are flared and his eyes are wide.

There is even a feeling of promised light in the sky, light that has not yet come but will spread out soon enough, open and vast and announce a morn. But not yet.

Growls from unseen parts of the woods – what is that, what is that larger thing? – a look of concern draws across the face of the sword-bearer, he knows he will have to fast locate the other two and get back to the house; he has sensed threat, he must get back. Fast.

Pete pushes on. Pushes himself. Determination in every fibre – he will find them, he will. Then hell to pay. Then revenge. Then satisfaction. For what he is owed.

The couple catch a glimpse of the house again through the trees but they have no time to applaud their success … because he is suddenly there: Pete, band leader. Become unhinged.

How had he managed to circle back so quickly?

Because he knows these pathways better than they do. He was always going to return before them. Did they think they could outwit him? Outwit Pete? He knows these parts. Multitude of land.

And so here they are.

All three of them.

Standing in a clearing now.

Just standing there.

This Un-band.

For band means solidarity, band means…

He assumes the pose.

He swipes the air with his sword.

"Look powerful, don't I?"

He laughs the hyena laugh again and this begets a growl again. Where is that coming from? That guttural, deep snarl.

He has already taken care of Genki… is that just Genki's ghost?

He laughs once more. Hyena. Animal. Well, he is in the wild.

"Just let us go, Pete. We've done no wrong."

"No wrong? You've done everything wrong, you fucking cunts! You think you can just leave now, yeah, is that what you think? Get in the van and just drive away? Is that the plan?"

Maiko is shaking, she looks like she will faint. Her entire body moans to be out of there, moans, moans, moans.

She hears the growls too – does it smell her? That animal in the forest. Does it get a whiff of her scent, her sex, her sorrow?

Pete still holds his sword erect, and words he said earlier come back to haunt Jason: *If you're not going to use it, then don't hold it. You'll only look weak.*

He does not look weak now, Pete. He looks the absolute opposite, bearing down on the female of the band.

"You'll be first, my darling. Oh, sure, you have a lovely voice and you have sparkling white teeth and everything… even a gay boy could be persuaded to turn. Until you came along he was happy to kneel before me, you know. Did you know that? How he thrust himself into me?"

"Please Pete, you need help. Let's go back to the city… you two can make amends, still play music and I'll disappear, I'll…"

"Help? It's a bit late for that. And what will you do in the city, my dear? You've got no manager now to guide your career. Aw. You poor things. *For I have heard the slander of many: fear was on every side: while they took counsel together against me, they devised to take away my life.*"

A jackal-ish laugh. He's got the entire canine kingdom in his sneers.

A swing of the sword – he swipes the air.

Blood has made the circle on the white head more pronounced, and still he keeps on joking:

"Just…I'm not really sure Genki has the head for business anymore. Do you get that joke, Maiko? *The head* for business!"

Swordswing.

Air.

Again, swiping nothing but air and the whipping sounds it makes.

"Stop, Pete. Put it down. Let me come to you."

Jason holds his own hands up, a gesture of defeat, of complete and utter surrender. He takes a step closer to him.

Growls, from somewhere…nearer.

Something is approaching all right, growing in growls. Closer.

Jason spots something on the ground then, just a few feet behind Pete – if he could just waltz him back to that. To that thing. It is not an animal. It's not that. It's maybe worse.

Pete is suspicious, but Jason keeps at it.

"Just put down the weapon, Pete, and let me come closer to you. Let me hold you. I promise we can make this work. Just me and you. Trust me."

Maiko lets Jason work his magic; she too has her suspicions…but she too has Genki's words rattling around inside of her: *Whatever mad game all this is, we have to play along. We must make sure he thinks that all is going according to his plan.*

Pete drops the sword and lets a huge smile overtake him.

"*The thief cometh not, but for to steal, and to kill, and to destroy.*"

But perhaps this is no thief after all.

He could let him in.

Pete could let Jason in again.

If they could just destroy that woman, that bitch, that usurper…then they could get back to normal. Things could get better. There could be music again.

Growls grow even closer.

And Jason takes one step nearer, hands outstretched, a man of peace; if he had a white flag he'd wave it, bears no ill will. Trust him.

"Genki's ghost," Pete laughs once more to himself.

"Just forgive me, Pete. I was wrong. Wrong to doubt you. Just let us go."

Jason steps right in front of Pete, and Maiko watches on, her heart in her throat, sweat out of every pore. She has seen it too, on the ground, and she knows what will happen next. She watches, avidly.

When he is directly in front of Pete, inches from him, just inches, he opens his arms wide for embrace, and Pete can no longer resist.

He allows himself to enter into this comforting fold, and he weeps for the sheer wonderment of it. Pete believes he has been saved. This is some kind of resurrection for him, an opening of that great rock, and for him to rise again. Trust. Trust.

But his wonderment is short-lived, for at that moment, Jason's ploy becomes plain, becomes plan.

His strong Montana hands, he places them on Pete's chest and he pushes the band leader back. Hard. With vigour. Deliberately. Hard.

And Pete stumbles.

Pete falls.

And with his wayward arm flailing out it sets off the trap that had been lying on the forest floor all along; waiting mechanical teeth; and the guitar-strumming arm of the mad musician gets caught in the iron clamp.

Snap!

Crunch!

The jagged jaws clasp around his forearm and the howls outroar even Maiko's previous caterwauls, and all horror is loosed among the trees.

The couple turn to each other, turn to each other and turn to run.

For a brief second though, Maiko, seeing the blood spurt from the writhing man, thinks they should stay and try save him.

But brief is all this moment is, for listen ... hark ... pay heed ...

Something is edging closer to their scene; it is very nearly upon them.

Something sniffs and slobbers, something knowing an easy meal is on the cards.

The couple have no choice but to bolt, and they do so, with all the speed they can muster, and without guilt, which they've left with the blood and the tears and the agony.

They do not look back to see the rictus of torture on the face of their once-friend, nor do they see the large and burly beast that approaches him, with more jaws, and with hard and swiping claws, and with ravenous intent.

43

The house says nothing – what more is left to say? – it just watches two of them draw near. It will not let them enter; when they try, when they try to move close to the front of it, the house begins a rumble.

In fact, the whole earth beneath their feet has started to reverberate, shaking the bodies of the already rattled duo, almost knocking them to the ground.

Earthquake.

"Have you got the keys?" she asks.

"They're still in the van."

They climb in and start the engine, this time to fully and properly escape. It has been the only thing on their mind, and now, at last it seems like they may be able to achieve it.

They cannot return to retrieve their equipment because the house is falling down around itself. It has given up. It has had quite enough. It would even say so, were it not crumbling to bits, shaken furiously by the land, being destroyed.

The house may not even mind so much. If the house, in the midst of its demolition, could talk, it might say: I have seen enough, far, far too much; I really don't really mind at all. This is the end.

<h1 style="text-align:center">44</h1>

A team of forensic detectives dig in the woods. They have been given clues. Maiko has told them about the gooseberry bush, and someone commented on how strange it was for such a bush to be growing there.

When plants that are not native start to encroach on other native plants of an area … they call that … invasive. Some plants are invasive.

Maiko did not see what they unearthed: a body, and an unconnected skull, another clear decapitation, the police team said.

Subsequent investigations revealed that the young man's name had been Haruki Kitsukawa. And that he'd been under the gooseberry bush for quite some time.

They were both offered counselling. Maiko and Jason. They both refused. They said they had music to make.

If they could think of three words that would define their new collection of tracks, the words would be: *horror, calamity, endure.*

45

Maiko moans on stage. It is just as she had promised herself. There is no point in even singing; words don't come easily to her anymore, in any language, it is best to not sing actual words at all, who needs them? Better to just moan them out instead, an expulsion, almost like the growls she heard in the forest that last time, that last time Pete lay and roared in final agony, his arm caught in the jaws of a trap he probably had set himself, and something had approached them, something nearing to their clearing, they could sense it in the rustling of the bushes; things were always on the move out there, from the very large down to the very small – she'd heard that growling, that snarl too, that hunger on the move and drawing close. Those are the moans she makes now, echoing all of that.

They are on stage.

Jason is surrounded by racks of synthesizers, computers, everything that is needed to make electronic/ambient music. There are electric guitars there too, should he feel the need, but he tends not to, they just remind him; he does not harp on about the glory days of rock and roll, and no longer does he mention erstwhile heroes. He hardly speaks at all. Just to confirm things with her: whether they are on the right track, musically, whether they are in tune, in the right key.

They are no longer lovers. They are in this for the money. This is their last chance to try and make some of it. Make something of themselves. Make a career. Make.

A few producers enjoy what they do, and say they might be useful for film soundtracks, scores for documentaries, perhaps, or horror films, yes, probably something along those lines, horror: the sounds they make. Horror sounds? They are practically experts.

The long-haired vocalist stands a few feet in front of him, her eyes closed and her mouth close to the microphone.

The crowd is there to watch her, to sway along to her moans, and they seem to moan right along, too. Even though these people do not know the reasons for her moans, they seem to get it, on some deep, intuitive level, yes. They seem to get it because they know fear, and they know strangeness, and they know shock and sadness and loss and love and lust and fetishes and a whole plethora of emotions that they can't particularly name either, but they can somehow feel. So, they just moan right along with her.

They do not know that as she stands there, Maiko is moaning about: a girl called Sayuri, her hunched shoulders and turned-in feet, her thick lips frozen in time and forever waiting there in a youth's bedroom, waiting to be kissed; about an old couple copulating behind a farm shed and their laughter; about the tart taste of gooseberries; about idioms and phrases that confuse; cicadas and crickets, or were they katydids; about white rooms and magic boxes and sharp swords; about disappearing children and freezers full of eyeballs; about storms that make a house shake and a man with no head bleeding out from the neck amongst hoes and hoses; about the heat, and the cold, and the heat, and the cold; about period pains and the calendar's hold; about fathers stomping upstairs during foreign dramas; about jobs and jobs and jobs; about disappointments; about Naomi fighting her, two friends pulling on each other's braids and a mother there watching hand over mouth; about hard wooden school chairs and boredom; about boxy bedrooms and boxy apartments; about the cruelty of cities, the savagery of the countryside; about sweat and angst and confusion, the ever-confusion of being alive; about religion and philosophy and remembering what other people have said or have written and how these things keep revolving inside your head.

The name of the group has been decided.

They do not say *band*, for *band* suggests solidarity, suggests togetherness.

The name of the group is The Deeper Natures. It is a kind of tribute. Both of them agreed on this, though they did not discuss it in any detail. It just seemed apt.

At the front of the stage, right before Maiko's feet, there is a rough doormat. In English it says: *Welcome.* This is for the audience, and for their world, or for an audience to enter their world, and God help anyone who turns it around.

When they leave the stage, the applause is usually fierce and heavy. Jason and Maiko always close their eyes for this, for an instant, and they think it sounds like country rain outside a house in the country, not a *country house*.

They tell the people in the darkness out there, they tell the darkness; they say that it was great to be there, and what a joy it was to moan for them, and with them, alongside them, and that they'll be back again soon.

Acknowledgments and thanks

To:
Tanja
Maria
John
Svetlana

You rock.

And to my family, ever patient, ever supportive, much love.

About the author

Colin O'Sullivan lives and works in the north of Japan with his family.

Colin O'Sullivan's first novel, *Killarney Blues*, captivated critics and readers alike and won the prestigious Prix Mystère de la Critique in France.

His second novel, a literary dystopia called *The Starved Lover Sings*, was published in Russia to critical acclaim.

His third novel, The *Dark Manual*, has been republished by Harper Collins under the name *Sunny* and made into a TV series by Apple TV.

O'Sullivan's short fiction and poetry have been published in various print and online anthologies and magazines.

To learn more about Colin O'Sullivan, please visit our website: www.betimesbooks.com.

Also from Betimes Books

Catherine Dunne
A Good Enough Mother

Abel Posse
A Long Day in Venice

Dimitri Bortnikov
Soul Catcher

Fionnuala Brennan
*The Painter's Women:
Goya in Light and Shade*

Hadley Colt
Permanent Fatal Error
The Red-Handed League

Les Edgetron
The Death of Tarpons

Sam Hawken
La Frontera

David Hogan
The Last Island

Hear Us Fade

Kim Hood
They All Fall Down

Richard Kalich
Central Park West Trilogy
The Assisted Living
Facility Library
A Man Made Long Ago

Robert Kalich
David Lazar

Patricia Ketola
Dirty Pictures

Jackie Mallon
Silk for the Feed Dogs

Donald Finnaeus Mayo
Francesca
The Insider's Guide to
Betrayal

Craig McDonald
One True Sentence
Forever's Just Pretend
Toros & Torsos
Roll the Credits
The Great Pretender
The Running Kind
Head Games
Print the Legend

Death in the Face
Three Chords & the Truth
Borderland Noir (editor)

Sean Moncrieff
The Angel of the Streetlamps

Colin O'Sullivan
Killarney Blues
The Starved Lover Sings
My Perfect Cousin
Marshmallows

Gérard Ramon
In Love with Paris

Kevin Stevens
Reach the Shining River